T0356874

LOVERS OF FRANZ K.

LOVERS OF

FRANZ

K.

B U R H A N
S Ö N M E Z

Translated from the Kurdish by
Sami Hêzil

Other Press
New York

Originally published in Kurdish as *Evîndarên Franz K.* in 2024
by Lîs Yayınevi, Diyarbakır, Turkey

Aragon's poem in the last chapter has been translated from the French
by Antonia Phinnemore: Louis Aragon, *Elsa* (Paris: Gallimard, 1959)

Production editor: Yvonne E. Cárdenas
Text designer: Patrice Sheridan
This book was set in Times New Roman by
Alpha Design & Composition of Pittsfield, NH

1 3 5 7 9 10 8 6 4 2

Library of Congress Cataloging-in-Publication Data
Names: Sönmez, Burhan, author. | Hêzil, Samî, 1975- translator.
Title: Lovers of Franz K. : a novel / Burhan Sönmez ; translated from the
Kurdish by Sami Hêzil.
Other titles: Evîndarên Franz K. English
Description: New York : Other Press, 2025.
Identifiers: LCCN 2024032069 (print) | LCCN 2024032070 (ebook) |
ISBN 9781635425376 (hardcover) | ISBN 9781635425383 (ebook)
Subjects: LCGFT: Thrillers (Fiction) | Novels.
Classification: LCC PK6908.9.S66 E9513 2025 (print) |
LCC PK6908.9.S66 (ebook) | DDC [FIC]—dc23
LC record available at https://lccn.loc.gov/2024032069
LC ebook record available at https://lccn.loc.gov/2024032070

You loved him when he was alive and you loved
him after. If you love him, it is not a sin to kill him.
Or is it more?

—ERNEST HEMINGWAY, *THE OLD MAN AND THE SEA*

What! Would you burn my books?

—CERVANTES, *DON QUIXOTE*

LOVERS OF FRANZ K.

1 WEST BERLIN POLICE STATION

Berlin is a city divided by a wall down the middle. People living there in the summer of 1968 are staring at the long wall and are complaining of the weather getting warmer and the buses running late.

The interrogation room in the basement of the police station on Friesenstraße is cool. Stone walls spread damp in the room.

Commissioner Müller sits across from the suspect, Ferdy Kaplan, lighting a cigarette and blowing out the smoke. He mutters to himself as he examines the papers spread out on the desk.

COMMISSIONER MÜLLER: "Yes, the name used in the passport—"

FERDY KAPLAN: "Used? That is my real name, Ferdy Kaplan. But it does not matter."

COMMISSIONER MÜLLER: "What does not matter?"

FERDY KAPLAN: "My name..."

COMMISSIONER MÜLLER: "Why not?"

FERDY KAPLAN: "The explanation is in the papers in front of you. There you can find the answers to your questions."

COMMISSIONER MÜLLER: "If only it were so, Mr. Kaplan. We will get answers to some questions from you. Won't we, boys?"

(The other three police officers in the room laugh.)

FERDY KAPLAN: "You want to know where I got the gun, and from whom, don't you?"

COMMISSIONER MÜLLER: "We will get there. According to the file here, you are staying in the Steglitz neighborhood. Your mother is German, your father is Turkish. You seem to live in Istanbul, and you frequently visit Paris. First, tell me when you arrived in Berlin."

FERDY KAPLAN: "I was born here. I am from here. Do not speak to me as if I were a foreigner."

COMMISSIONER MÜLLER: "You are from here, but mostly you live elsewhere."

FERDY KAPLAN: "That is not a crime. If you had lived in other places, perhaps you would have found yourself better professions."

(Ferdy Kaplan looks toward the police officer taking notes at the next table.)

COMMISSIONER MÜLLER: "We have no complaints about our profession. We are in a better situation than you. Think about yourself, not us."

FERDY KAPLAN: "I'm happy with the chair I am in."

COMMISSIONER MÜLLER: "How can you be so sure of yourself?"

FERDY KAPLAN: "I can tell you if you would like to hear."

COMMISSIONER MÜLLER: "Oh, can you?"

FERDY KAPLAN: "Yes, let me explain."

COMMISSIONER MÜLLER: "Well then..."

FERDY KAPLAN: "Where would you like me to start?"

COMMISSIONER MÜLLER: "Why don't you start with your origin? *Kaplan* is a Jewish name..."

FERDY KAPLAN: No, it is a popular surname in Turkey. It means *tiger* in Turkish."

3

COMMISSIONER MÜLLER: Tell me about your mother and father... People like you are rare."

FERDY KAPLAN: "What do you mean?"

COMMISSIONER MÜLLER: "Suspects are mostly tight-lipped; they are not inclined to speak openly."

FERDY KAPLAN: "People with no beliefs behave that way; they are afraid of talking."

COMMISSIONER MÜLLER: "Is there a belief in committing a crime?"

FERDY KAPLAN: "I don't think that I committed a crime, I only did what I believed in. I did what had to be done."

COMMISSIONER MÜLLER: "You did 'what had to be done,' is that so? Honestly, I am curious now how you are going to explain all of this."

FERDY KAPLAN: "Everything I will mention is available in your records, you don't need to take notes. *(Ferdy Kaplan glances at the police officer at the next table taking notes.)* My mother was a Nazi supporter. My Turkish father shared the same ideas. They died here during a Soviet bombardment in the last days of the war. My grandfather rescued me out of the ruins. When he fell ill with his kidneys, he must have realized a year later that he wouldn't live long and sent me off to my father's family in Istanbul."

For a boy of ten, who had come from the rubble and ruin of Berlin, Istanbul was a magical place. Ferdy looked up at the ever-changing colors of the sky between the towers, domes, and city walls. He immersed himself in the bustling bazaars and saw the joy on people's faces. He listened to the sound of horse-drawn carriages, suburban trains, and ferryboats. The sea, which he could not dream of during the war, was on one side, and his grandparents were on the other. There was no fear of death. His grandfather and grandmother embraced their grandson as if he were a gift from God. They made him a bed on the floor in their own room. At night they would tell him fairy tales they had once told to their own son and listened to Ferdy's familiar breathing.

As Ferdy grew better at speaking Turkish, he put up with the ridicule of some kids at school and the excessive attention of others. His German identity brought together two opposing sides of his life. His closest friend was Amalya. Unlike other girls, she would confront boys and protect Ferdy. Sometimes she would walk all the way home with him. One day, when one of Ferdy's headaches returned, they sat down among the trees. Amalya touched Ferdy's right temple, then kissed him on the cheek. It took a week for Ferdy to show the same courage and return the kiss. They often played away from the other children. They would hide among the rocks on the Kumkapı shore or in the old city walls at the Yedikule vegetable gardens. They would sing songs and read books together. Ferdy began to draw pictures again. He would draw fishing boats, the flocks of seagulls, and the setting sun. Amalya would ask why his drawings didn't look like normal pictures. The boats would be awry, the wings of seagulls broken, and the sunlight blurred. Ferdy drew Amalya's smiling face, her serene face, her sleepy face.

When Amalya was fifteen she moved to France with her mother. (As Ferdy Kaplan recounts his story, he makes no mention of Amalya.) Ferdy's grandfather passed away the same year. His heart had suddenly stopped while he was in conversation with a customer at his fish stall in Kumkapı. They buried him in the cemetery by the old city walls at Topkapı. In the first year after he died, Ferdy and his grandmother visited his grave every Friday. Later on, they would visit him twice a year, on religious festivals. Life was fast-flowing, Ferdy was trying to keep up with this pace and grow up as quickly as possible. He would go to school in the mornings and help his grandmother in the fish stall in the afternoons. He began to learn about politics, overhearing the conversations of fishermen. The party founded by the conservatives had come to power. The political arena of the country was in disarray with bridges being broken between the government and the opposition party. Nobody could realize they were on a path leading to a military coup. Amalya, who had left the country when the new government was formed, returned after ten years to find the government shaken to its foundations. This was right at the peak of the protests. Despite the passing of ten years, Ferdy recognized Amalya in the crowd when he saw her at one of the demonstrations.

COMMISSIONER MÜLLER: "How did the political turmoil affect your life? Perhaps it became the reason that led to your presence here in a police station."

FERDY KAPLAN: "Everything had an effect on me: the war that ruined Germany, the political unrest that shook Turkey, the events that stirred France entirely—"

COMMISSIONER MÜLLER: "France, yes. Were you in Paris during the protests in May?"

FERDY KAPLAN: "Everybody was there."

COMMISSIONER MÜLLER: "So, when did you come here?"

FERDY KAPLAN: "I came a week ago."

COMMISSIONER MÜLLER: "That's interesting. How could you leave and come to Berlin while Paris was boiling up with the mad fever of youth? Why?"

FERDY KAPLAN: "But isn't it, in your words, boiling up here too?"

COMMISSIONER MÜLLER: "Did you return for that reason?"

FERDY KAPLAN: "You don't need a reason to come home."

COMMISSIONER MÜLLER: "If you killed someone, well, you will need a reason."

FERDY KAPLAN: "I come to Berlin every year."

COMMISSIONER MÜLLER: "So did you come here directly, or did you stop off first in East Berlin?"

FERDY KAPLAN: "No, I did not go to East Berlin at all."

COMMISSIONER MÜLLER: "You mean you have not been there in your whole life?"

FERDY KAPLAN: "Since Berlin was divided, I have never been to the East."

COMMISSIONER MÜLLER: "Why? Having grown up in this city, have you never wondered how things are on the other side?"

FERDY KAPLAN: "When I come to Berlin I stay on this side of the border. Our house is here. My grandfather's grave is here."

COMMISSIONER MÜLLER: "Your neighborhood is close to the border, but you haven't thought about crossing to the other side. Do you expect us to believe that?"

FERDY KAPLAN: "I expect nothing from you."

COMMISSIONER MÜLLER: "You killed a student, Mr. Kaplan. We will see in what way it is related to the border and the other side of the Wall."

FERDY KAPLAN: "It has nothing to do with the border and the Wall."

COMMISSIONER MÜLLER: "It is our job to assume the opposite of what you are telling us."

FERDY KAPLAN: "I am telling you the truth. That is as true as my identity and the offense I accept responsibility for."

COMMISSIONER MÜLLER: "If so, why did you kill the student?"

FERDY KAPLAN: "Why do you keep calling him 'the student,' doesn't he have a name?"

COMMISSIONER MÜLLER: "Don't you know who he is? Are you a hired killer, who murders people unknown to you?"

FERDY KAPLAN: "I don't kill anybody for money."

COMMISSIONER MÜLLER: "What would you kill for?"

FERDY KAPLAN: "Can I have a cigarette?"

COMMISSIONER MÜLLER: "Later. For now, let's see how events developed. *(Commissioner Müller turns to the bearded police officer who is standing by the wall.)* You tell us how it happened."

BEARDED POLICE OFFICER: "Yesterday evening, I was in front of the central library. I heard screams from the bus station across the street. I ran over. I saw this man and a woman with him, both were holding guns. They shot a university student waiting at the bus stop. The student fell to the ground, lifeless. An elderly man at the bus stop was also injured in the gunfire. When I shouted, the attackers started running. I followed and caught up with them. When Ferdy Kaplan realized they could not escape me, he stood behind a tree and shot at me. He wanted to give the woman with him a chance to disappear. I took cover behind the wall of a building, protected myself, and shot at him. When he ran out of bullets, I went over and captured him. By this time the woman had run away."

COMMISSIONER MÜLLER: "Is this how it happened?"

FERDY KAPLAN: "How can it be possible that your officer sees so clearly in the dark? His story has no credibility. I was alone there. I don't know the woman who was running beside me. She must be someone who had panicked and started running."

BEARDED POLICE OFFICER: "We collected the bullet casings, and the total number exceeds the ones in your gun's magazine. That means not one gun was used but two. The other gun was on that woman, wasn't it?"

FERDY KAPLAN: "I had two guns. When the bullets of the first gun ran out, I threw it into the bushes and used the second one."

BEARDED POLICE OFFICER: "We searched every corner, but we couldn't find any other gun. We are sure that woman was with you."

FERDY KAPLAN: "If you are so sure, then speak to her."

BEARDED POLICE OFFICER: "We will speak to her when we catch her."

FERDY KAPLAN: "That means you couldn't catch her…"

(The room falls into silence. They all look at one another.)

COMMISSIONER MÜLLER: "We will soon find her and we will question her in this room too."

FERDY KAPLAN: "You are wasting your time."

COMMISSIONER MÜLLER: "Don't bother yourself with our time."

FERDY KAPLAN: "If you are using your time wisely, then how come you cannot yet identify who that young student was?"

COMMISSIONER MÜLLER: "How come you think that we don't know who he was? We know, as you do, his name was Ernest Fischer. Regarding his studies, he was a good student. We have gathered that he had participated in a couple of demonstrations, but he doesn't seem to be so prominent a person as to be a target of such an attack. Is there anything you can tell us about him that we don't yet know?"

FERDY KAPLAN: "I would tell you if I knew."

COMMISSIONER MÜLLER: "Did you get involved in the other attacks against students? For example, the attack that took place in April."

FERDY KAPLAN: "Do you mean the attack in which Rudi Dutschke was injured? The suspect in that attack was caught, isn't that so?"

COMMISSIONER MÜLLER: "Then you must also have known the student who was killed last year."

FERDY KAPLAN: "Benno Ohnesorg, yes."

COMMISSIONER MÜLLER: "I see you are very interested in these incidents."

FERDY KAPLAN: "It's not unusual, every detail appeared in the press, even newspapers in Paris and Istanbul reported the incident."

COMMISSIONER MÜLLER: "That's right, it made a little too much noise."

FERDY KAPLAN: "But weren't the police the perpetrators of the murder last year?"

COMMISSIONER MÜLLER: "It may seem so, but we suspect that there must be some network behind that incident that we are not fully aware of yet."

FERDY KAPLAN: "It's good that you suspect an unknown network of your own officers. But it was your attack on the student demonstrations that led to all this. Because the students were protesting against the Shah of Iran, you turned it into a battlefield. When the dictator of Iran attended a performance of Mozart's *Magic Flute* at the Alte Oper, you were fully at his service."

COMMISSIONER MÜLLER: "Our duty is to maintain public order, so that people can continue their daily lives."

FERDY KAPLAN: "Is that why you killed a student?"

COMMISSIONER MÜLLER: "Why did you kill a student, Mr. Kaplan?"

FERDY KAPLAN: "These are two completely different things."

COMMISSIONER MÜLLER: "Oh, of course, you killed him on purpose, you did it in a prepared and studied manner. In this case, they are entirely different things."

FERDY KAPLAN: "If you knew the content of the matter, you wouldn't talk like that."

COMMISSIONER MÜLLER: "That's right. It is the content of the matter. Explain that to us."

FERDY KAPLAN: "All the explanations you need are written on the papers in front of you."

COMMISSIONER MÜLLER: "No, there is no information here other than the normal life of a student. You must tell us, what was special about this young man that we couldn't yet figure out?"

FERDY KAPLAN: "I only know what is already known to you. I don't know anything else."

COMMISSIONER MÜLLER: "Well, you keep up your little act. We looked into Ernest Fischer's political connections. We established that he was not a member of the Student Union of German Socialists. We don't know if he joined an illegal group that was newly formed, which we haven't been able to identify yet. We are investigating his possible connections with the previously murdered students. As soon as we get the first piece of evidence, we will see how you are linked to those attacks. I believe that your crimes go that far."

FERDY KAPLAN: "Do your research well. Then you will see that I have nothing to do with these two other events. I was not here on those days. You can check the records of my entering and leaving the country."

COMMISSIONER MÜLLER: "Ernest Fischer's father and mother both work in the iron factory. Ernest was a good student, loved very much by his friends. I was wondering if some kind of jealousy caused all this. Could your woman friend who escaped the scene have something to do with the murder?"

FERDY KAPLAN: "Nonsense."

COMMISSIONER MÜLLER: "So you must have a reason that is not nonsense. Why did you kill him?"

FERDY KAPLAN: "Can I have a cigarette?"

COMMISSIONER MÜLLER: "It seems obvious that you will not confess. But at the beginning, I thought you would speak openly."

FERDY KAPLAN: "I told you what I know. How can I tell you things that I don't know?"

COMMISSIONER MÜLLER: "We will find out soon. We are investigating whether Ernest Fischer, or his family, has any connection with Turkey too."

FERDY KAPLAN: "That is a waste of time."

COMMISSIONER MÜLLER: "Then tell us how not to waste our time."

FERDY KAPLAN: "Well, let me tell you: Step away from the points you are focusing on, forget the questions you asked me. If you avoid making these mistakes, you will save time."

COMMISSIONER MÜLLER: "These words of yours are not very reliable. You must try a little harder to convince us."

FERDY KAPLAN: "Okay, continue researching old murders, follow the connections to East Berlin and Istanbul. You know best. But you won't find a single crumb."

COMMISSIONER MÜLLER: "I really wanted to believe you."

FERDY KAPLAN: "Let's see when you finally realize that I am telling you the truth."

COMMISSIONER MÜLLER: "Do not doubt our abilities, Mr. Kaplan."

FERDY KAPLAN: "Was that Fischer, the student's name? Please pass on my condolences to his mother and father. Can you do that for me?"

COMMISSIONER MÜLLER: "Are you offering condolences? To the family of the person you killed."

FERDY KAPLAN: "Yes."

COMMISSIONER MÜLLER: "You cannot be in your right mind."

FERDY KAPLAN: "No, I'm quite all right, that's why I offer my condolences to the Fischer family. But, after all, it won't mean much, unfortunately."

COMMISSIONER MÜLLER: "How strange..."

2 WEST BERLIN COURTROOM

Fearing unrest may erupt due to an armed attack on a student, the police announce to the press that this was a crime of passion. In reality, they are considering various options for a concrete clue, including a link with East Germany or the youth protests in France.

One week later, Ferdy Kaplan is taken from Tegel Prison to the courthouse in Moabit. He is brought before a panel of three judges. The lead judge confirms his identity, and then he gives the floor to the prosecutor.

PROSECUTOR: "Your Honor! The defendant, Ferdy Kaplan, was arrested for the murder of a twenty-year-old student. The brave officers of our police force caught him red-handed on the spot, but we still don't know the motive for the attack. Whether we figure out the reason or not, the death of Ernest Fischer is a fact. The defendant, Ferdy Kaplan—"

JUDGE: "Has the defendant admitted to the murder charge?"

PROSECUTOR: "Yes."

FERDY KAPLAN: "Yes."

JUDGE: "Mr. Kaplan, I didn't ask you. You are the defendant. You will not speak without my permission."

FERDY KAPLAN: "I didn't actually respond to you, I only… *(Ferdy Kaplan turns toward the public gallery and looks at a couple sitting hand in hand, an expression of weariness on their faces.)* With your permission, I would like to offer my condolences to the family of the young man who died. You must be the Fischer family… *(The middle-aged man and woman lift their gazes and give him a sorrowful look.)* Mrs. Fischer! Mr. Fischer! I am very sorry for the death of your son. Please accept my sincere apologies."

(Tears fill Mrs. Fischer's eyes. Her husband puts his arm around her shoulders.)

PROSECUTOR: "This is ridiculous, Your Honor! The defendant wants to turn this courtroom into a theater."

FERDY KAPLAN: "I would act much better if I wanted to. I just expressed my genuine sadness. I have no expectation that your court will approve of my feelings. If Mr. and Mrs. Fischer believe me just a little, then that will be enough for me. I am a man of truth, not a man of tricks."

PROSECUTOR: "A man of truth? You?"

FERDY KAPLAN: "Yes, me."

JUDGE: "That's enough, defendant! I warn you. I don't want any play in my court. The case will proceed by the rules."

FERDY KAPLAN: "Your Honor, I am not trying to cause trouble. But I would like it recorded that I bow my head in respect for the young soul of Ernest Fischer."

(Ferdy Kaplan looks at the court clerk sitting across from him. The court clerk stops writing for a moment, waiting for confirmation from the judge.)

JUDGE: "Don't worry. Whatever you say will be recorded."

(The clattering of the typewriter starts again.)

FERDY KAPLAN: "Also..."

JUDGE: "Yes?"

FERDY KAPLAN: "I have been incarcerated for a week, even though I asked for a cigarette my request was ignored."

JUDGE: "During a break in the hearing you may smoke a cigarette. *(The judge turns to the court usher and gives him instructions.)* Now, Mr. Kaplan, you are hereby being tried for murder. This is a serious case. Be quiet and await your turn."

FERDY KAPLAN: "Of course. I can assure you that it will be a proper hearing."

JUDGE: "Now, Mr. Prosecutor, please continue. You were talking about the student..."

PROSECUTOR: "Ernest Fischer, he was a student at the Free University of Berlin, studying at the Institute of Biology."

JUDGE: "On the day of the incident there was no student protest, am I right?"

PROSECUTOR: "That is correct, Your Honor. Although school was on a holiday, almost every day there were protests, but on the day of the incident it was quiet. Ernest Fischer went to the library in the morning and studied there until evening. When he left the library, he went to the bus stop opposite and waited for his bus."

JUDGE: "Was he alone? Any friend..."

PROSECUTOR: "He was alone, but there were two assailants. Besides the defendant, Ferdy Kaplan, there was a woman. We haven't ascertained her identity yet. She took advantage of the darkness and escaped. She was in her thirties, had short hair—"

FERDY KAPLAN: "Mr. Prosecutor."

PROSECUTOR: "Yes?"

FERDY KAPLAN: "I wish you would concentrate your efforts in the right direction rather than giving your attention to the hair color of someone who has no connection with me. You are being neglectful by looking at the shooter instead of looking at the victim."

PROSECUTOR: "We are not here to play with words. Either you identify your accomplice, or you will face the fullest extent of justice."

FERDY KAPLAN: "Justice..."

PROSECUTOR: "Are you belittling it? Killing a student and injuring an old man are not crimes that we belittle in the court of justice."

FERDY KAPLAN: "No, I never discredit justice. I always believe in it."

PROSECUTOR: "We are giving you the opportunity to be open here. Tell us, in the presence of the court and the victim's family, why did you commit this murder, who were your collaborators, and who was the woman with you during the assault?"

FERDY KAPLAN: "You keep circling around the same narrow spot. Anything I say will not contribute to your conclusions."

PROSECUTOR: "Try, if you will. Try to tell us something we don't know, though."

FERDY KAPLAN: "Well, then, I will tell you if you want to hear that badly."

PROSECUTOR: "Please, if you could..."

FERDY KAPLAN: "Someone was wounded at the scene, right?"

PROSECUTOR: "The elderly man."

FERDY KAPLAN: "Yes, him."

PROSECUTOR: "Well, what about it?"

FERDY KAPLAN: "Do you have a description of him in your notes?"

PROSECUTOR: "A description?"

FERDY KAPLAN: "Yes, like him having a humpback, for example?"

PROSECUTOR: "Humpback? *(The prosecutor glances at the papers in front of him.)* What's the importance of that?"

FERDY KAPLAN: "But you are assuming that the short hair of a woman who panicked and ran away in the dark has importance, is that so?"

For research related to her PhD in urban architecture at the Sorbonne, Amalya returned to Istanbul, the city of her childhood. As soon as she arrived, instead of visiting the shores of the Bosphorus, she went to her old neighborhood. She saw that Kumkapı was demolished, torn apart from right to left. The fishermen's market on the waterfront was erased and an asphalt road spread out in its place. The urban gardens under the city walls had been filled with newly constructed buildings. The color of the city had changed, the shade of the trees had vanished. "What have they done to my neighborhood?" Amalya came across a few old acquaintances among the concrete buildings that had replaced ornamented wooden houses. She found out that Ferdy's grandmother had died and Ferdy had left the neighborhood. What changes cities faster, when buildings are demolished or when friends are gone? Amalya wandered around for a few days, seeking the familiar scent of her childhood. She boarded the suburban train and traveled back and forth along the thousand-year-old city walls of Istanbul. While visiting Sirkeci, Samatya, and Bakırköy, she thought that the new developments not only erase the memories of the city but also annihilate the beauty of the city. She wrote a letter to her mother. "Eliz," she said, addressing her by her first name as usual, "if you want to die happy, never see the new face of Istanbul, rely on the things that you have in your memories."

On the day she sent the letter she came across a protest march. Young and old, men and women were advancing toward a square, and on the way their numbers grew. Amalya joined the crowd and chanted anti-government slogans, polishing her rusty Turkish by shouting alongside the people. The Istanbul she had left behind and the one she had returned to were two entirely different places. When the crowd flowed into Beyazıt Square, it sounded like a big forest. Amalya became part of a people whom she did not know. She swayed like all the others. When someone approached her from behind and grabbed her by the wrist, she was startled. At first, she thought it was a plainclothes policeman, then she recognized him. "Ferdy..." They didn't get a chance to speak in the sudden turmoil of the crowd. As a result of the police attack on the demonstration, one person died and many others were detained. The next morning, when they met, Amalya hugged Ferdy tightly and kissed him on the cheek, remembering their old days together.

It was then that she noticed the hesitancy in Ferdy's reaction and the engagement ring on his finger. Those were beautiful spring days. They wandered around together and visited places they both knew. Old locations. Old names. Stories and laughter. Who knew when they would meet again? Two days later, when she was leaving for Paris, Amalya looked forward to seeing Ferdy at the airport. Ferdy didn't turn up to see her off and say goodbye, even though he had promised that he would.

PROSECUTOR: "You avoid mentioning the name of the woman who was with you. You pretend that such a person doesn't exist. But we have witnesses to the incident and the bullet casings collected at the scene—"

FERDY KAPLAN: "And you are going after a woman who fled in the dark, while you don't know the person in front of you."

PROSECUTOR: "Who is it that we don't know? You?"

FERDY KAPLAN: "Oh God, look at these men who are trying me here! Is this what I deserve?"

PROSECUTOR: "Mr. Kaplan, your words—"

MRS. FISCHER: "Why my son? Why?"

(When they hear her voice, they all turn around and look at Mrs. Fischer. The courtroom is silent for a moment.)

FERDY KAPLAN: "For days, I have been wondering the same thing, Mrs. Fischer. I keep asking myself the same question: Why?"

MRS. FISCHER: "Every night I wait for my son, I keep expecting him to appear suddenly. But he doesn't. Damn you!"

FERDY KAPLAN: "I am sincerely apologizing to you, again."

MRS. FISCHER: "Why my son?"

FERDY KAPLAN: "I am going to write a letter to him."

MRS. FISCHER: "What letter are you talking about? You murderer!"

(Mrs. Fischer begins to sob loudly.)

PROSECUTOR: "Mrs. Fischer, our court will deliver justice. This man will receive the punishment he deserves."

MRS. FISCHER: "I don't care about justice. I want my son."

PROSECUTOR: "I understand your loss, your grief. But the pursuit of justice is the only thing that can lead us to the truth. Your son's soul, too, is looking forward to that truth."

MRS. FISCHER: "Mr. Prosecutor, when you mention the truth, I don't know what you mean. Will that bring my son back to me?"

PROSECUTOR: "I do understand your feelings, Mrs. Fischer—"

FERDY KAPLAN: "With your permission, may I ask Mrs. Fischer a question?"

(The prosecutor first looks at Ferdy Kaplan, then turns to the judge.)

PROSECUTOR: "Your Honor?"

JUDGE: "Yes, he may ask."

FERDY KAPLAN: "Thank you, Your Honor."

JUDGE: "Do keep it short."

FERDY KAPLAN: "Mrs. Fischer, why did you name your son Ernest? In Germany this name is spelled as *E r n s t*, it doesn't include the second *e*."

PROSECUTOR: "Mr. Kaplan…"

FERDY KAPLAN: "Yes?"

PROSECUTOR: "What kind of a question is this? Your manner is becoming more abnormal."

FERDY KAPLAN: "I assume it is an official duty of prosecutors to find defendants abnormal."

PROSECUTOR: "This question has no meaning. Mrs. Fischer is not obliged to answer it."

FERDY KAPLAN: "Every single letter of our names has a meaning. If only you knew how much I suffered for the sake of only one letter."

MR. FISCHER: "Mr. Prosecutor, if you permit me, I can explain."

PROSECUTOR: "All right, Mr. Fischer, please go ahead."

MR. FISCHER: "When my wife and I were newly married, we hid an American soldier in our home. It was the last year of the war. He had escaped from prison. As he was trying to escape, he was shot and injured. We did our best, but he only survived for a couple of weeks. His name was Ernest, or that was what he told us. When our son was born, we gave him that name."

FERDY KAPLAN: "Thank you, Mr. Fischer. I hope your son didn't suffer much due to that extra letter in his name."

MR. FISCHER: "What kind of suffering? I don't understand."

PROSECUTOR: "Mr. Kaplan, what is your intention? I am beginning to doubt your sanity. We came across such things in the other attacks against students. I may ask the court to refer you for a psychiatric examination."

FERDY KAPLAN: "You are confusing me with Bachmann?"

PROSECUTOR: "You are talking about the Bachmann who wounded the student leader Rudi Dutschke, aren't you? So, do you know him?"

FERDY KAPLAN: "No, I don't know him, I have heard his name. I don't want to be treated in the same way as some such person."

PROSECUTOR: "How do you know what kind of person he is?"

FERDY KAPLAN: "Is there anyone who doesn't know him?"

PROSECUTOR: "Are both of you members of the same organization?"

FERDY KAPLAN: "Mr. Prosecutor, your police officers have asked me this question several times."

PROSECUTOR: "But you did not give them any information."

FERDY KAPLAN: "What would I give them?"

PROSECUTOR: "Your methods and target resemble Bachmann's. Though he is not as successful as you."

FERDY KAPLAN: "Those are entirely different incidents. He is an anti-communist psychopath."

PROSECUTOR: "What about you then, what are you?"

FERDY KAPLAN: "I am neither an anti-communist nor a psychopath."

PROSECUTOR: "Those who commit murder always refute these kinds of arguments."

FERDY KAPLAN: "I told your police officers, and I will tell you too, that I consider every question on this subject to be an insult."

PROSECUTOR: "As you are trying to avoid the question, we may assume that you do have a connection with Bachmann."

FERDY KAPLAN: "I am not avoiding anything."

PROSECUTOR: "Well, this is a sensitive area. We will go deeper in our search. In a few days, when we obtain some concrete data, you will not be able to deny it so easily."

FERDY KAPLAN: "Search as much as you like, you will always be on the wrong track."

PROSECUTOR: "And which is the right track? You tell us, then, how can we find out the truth?"

FERDY KAPLAN: "As I said, you have no concrete evidence. All you need to do is to change your point of view."

PROSECUTOR: "Mr. Kaplan, please be more specific."

FERDY KAPLAN: "All right. First, take your focus away from me. Also take it away from the student who died. Try looking somewhere else."

PROSECUTOR: "Where else, for example? Shall we focus on your partner who escaped in the dark?"

FERDY KAPLAN: "The same tale, once again. While you are concerning yourself with an unknown woman, you have no idea about the humpbacked old man who was wounded."

PROSECUTOR: "You have already said this."

FERDY KAPLAN: "Let me tell you something new then, or rather, let me ask you."

PROSECUTOR: "What will you ask about?"

FERDY KAPLAN: "Mr. Prosecutor, you have no knowledge of what kind of man he was and you do not know his description. Do you even know his name?"

PROSECUTOR: "The wounded man?"

FERDY KAPLAN: "Yes."

PROSECUTOR: "His name... *(The prosecutor riffles through the papers before him, looking nervous.)* His name... I think he was a tourist—"

FERDY KAPLAN: "Brod."

PROSECUTOR: "Excuse me?"

FERDY KAPLAN: "The old man."

PROSECUTOR: "Do you know him?"

FERDY KAPLAN: "It seems as if you don't know who he is."

PROSECUTOR: "Now, it is here, I found it, Max Brod."

FERDY KAPLAN: "Fools."

3 WEST BERLIN
COURTROOM

When it becomes evident that the wounded man is a notable author, the prosecutor and the police spend the night assessing the new situation. They are making "urgent" coded phone calls to Tel Aviv, Istanbul, and Prague. Max Brod was born in Prague. When the Nazis occupied Prague about thirty years ago, he moved to Tel Aviv and settled there. He is now in Germany for a short visit to talk about his friend Franz Kafka. On his deathbed, Kafka left his notebooks and papers to Brod, with certain instructions in his will that all of them should be burned. Instead, Brod decided to publish all of Kafka's works.

Police are not giving Max Brod's name to the press. It is clear that West Germany, while trying to alleviate the suffering of the war, will be put in a difficult situation by the news of the shooting of an Israeli Jewish author whose books had previously been burned here. For this reason, there are no journalists at the hearing the next day.

JUDGE: "Mr. Kaplan, do you still stand by your decision not to hire a lawyer?"

FERDY KAPLAN: "I don't need any legal assistance. Thank you for asking."

JUDGE: "How does the prosecution view this decision?"

PROSECUTOR: "The defendant's decision stems from his self-confidence. Due to new information we have obtained since yesterday, we believe that he needs legal assistance more than before. However, it's his right under the law not to ask for a lawyer."

JUDGE: "You have not submitted the new findings you mention."

PROSECUTOR: "We were able to complete them just before the hearing began. Here they are, Your Honor."

JUDGE: "Well...that's all right...I see new allegations here. You may proceed."

PROSECUTOR: "The files contain information that the parents of the defendant were Nazi supporters and they both died in Berlin during the war. It is understood that the defendant was brought up by his parents until the age of nine, that he was influenced by their ideas and anti-Semitic sentiments. We now know that the target of the attack last week was, in fact, Max Brod. It appears that the student Ernest Fischer was killed by accident."

JUDGE: "Are you sure of that? Isn't it possible that both of those men were targeted? Maybe there is a connection between Ernest Fischer and Max Brod."

PROSECUTOR: "Along with our investigations here, we have also contacted the police in Tel Aviv and Prague. We have not received any information of a possible connection between Ernest Fischer and Mr. Brod."

JUDGE: "So, you mean to say that a young student lost his life through misfortune? Are you sure of that?"

PROSECUTOR: "Yes."

(Mrs. Fischer's cries are heard. Mr. Fischer takes her by the arm, and they exit the courtroom together.)

JUDGE: "What was Ernest Fischer's background? Was he also a Jew?"

PROSECUTOR: "We did some research on him as well. We checked the identity and immigration records and found no trace of Jews in the Fischer family. They are purely a German family."

JUDGE: "Purely... what do you mean by that?"

PROSECUTOR: "I mean, they are a normal German family with a Catholic background. Originally, they are from Frankfurt, and they migrated to Berlin three generations ago."

JUDGE: "Does this mean that the attack on Max Brod was carried out with racist motives?"

PROSECUTOR: "That is what we think. It seems that an anti-Semitic group has begun a campaign of aggression against prominent writers and intellectuals, and they picked Max Brod as their first target. It would be a good start for them. Mr. Brod is someone who fled the Nazis during the war and settled in present-day Israel. Besides his writing, he is recognized for his dedication to the Zionist ideal."

JUDGE: "Of these two characteristics, his writing and his Zionism, am I to understand it was the latter that made him a target?"

PROSECUTOR: "That is how we view it, Your Honor. Mr. Brod is committed to his faith and his nation. He believes that the land of Palestine is the historic land that was promised to them. This makes him a good target for the Aryan supremacist groups."

JUDGE: "Why was Berlin chosen as the place for the attack?"

PROSECUTOR: "We think that the attack was carried out here to revive memories of Germany's past. They would either take revenge in this way for the defeat in the war or show that the war was not yet over and the Aryan ideology has not been defeated. It was a new message of hope for Germans living with the old dream, and we know such people exist."

JUDGE: "When you think of it that way, Berlin seems to have been a good choice. How did they know that Mr. Brod was coming here?"

PROSECUTOR: "Before he arrived, Mr. Brod announced his travel plans and his schedule."

JUDGE: "He was an old man, over eighty. What if he'd changed his mind at the last minute, and if he'd decided not to come—"

PROSECUTOR: "You are right, he came here despite his health concerns. If he had not come, we believe that another Jewish intellectual in West Germany would have been targeted."

JUDGE: "And they sent a half German, half Turkish man who was living in Istanbul to accomplish this attack, wasn't it so?"

PROSECUTOR: "It seems the attacker has sentiments of personal revenge. The death of both of his parents in the war—"

FERDY KAPLAN: "Mr. Prosecutor—"

JUDGE: "Wait a moment, Mr. Kaplan, let Mr. Prosecutor finish, I will come to you."

PROSECUTOR: "We contacted the Turkish police forces. They said that Ferdy Kaplan participated in the protests against the right-wing government in 1960, but after that he was not part of any active movement and had no affiliations with leftist associations or parties. They assume that while he was living a quiet and ordinary life, he actually joined right-wing and racist groups. They will provide us with detailed information of their intelligence within a few days."

JUDGE: "Is it possible that the defendant has links to Palestinian militants? You know, since Israel defeated the Arab armies last year, there is violence spreading across Europe as well as the region. We hear of a new incident every other day."

PROSECUTOR: "This is something we are also looking into. We asked for information from the Israeli police on this matter."

FERDY KAPLAN: "Unrelated assumptions, irrelevant stories. Supposedly information will come from Turkish police...information will come from Israeli police...It's all meaningless..."

Most of the bodies that remained under the ruins in Berlin were never recovered. As the wailings from the ruins faded away a few days later, the smell of rotting flesh filled the air. Ferdy, too, trapped under a broken door, stopped moaning and lost consciousness. Having searched everywhere for him, when his grandfather finally found him, he could hardly recognize his grandson from the dried blood that covered his face. He cleaned Ferdy's eyes, mouth, and neck, and dripped water between his cracked lips. He took him on his back and carried him to the Red Army medical base. He spoke to the soldiers there in a way they understood, managing to convince them to help the boy. The medics wrapped Ferdy's head in a bandage and gave him some painkillers. They whispered to his grandfather that the boy's condition was not promising at all. On his grandfather's back, Ferdy returned to their half-destroyed home. He slept deliriously. For days he waited for his mother and father. Perhaps it was all a dream, and when he awoke, he would find them by his side. He often had the same dream during the war.

Ferdy slowly began to recover. He got used to his grandfather's cooking. He read the books he found in the rubble. His grandfather became his tutor. They read together and painted together. Before too long, they began to laugh together. That brought them closer. It was then that his grandfather spoke to Ferdy about a serious matter. He said he was not a Nazi and like many Germans he had to hide his ideas out of fear. He spoke of the evil of Nazism. Ferdy did not understand. He did not believe that his mother, his father, their neighbors, and even Hitler himself were wrong. Then, how could he be sure of the truth? He followed his grandfather who said, "We shall paint pictures, so we can forget and heal our wounds." With each color, he learned to see the beautiful soul at the heart of the ruins. While he looked at the destroyed buildings, he saw and painted lively houses and streets. After a year, his grandfather had yet another serious conversation with him. He said that he was getting old and soon he wouldn't be able to look after him anymore. He said that Ferdy had better go to his father's family in Istanbul and that he would be happier living there. After all, the situation in Berlin was obvious. Ferdy cried. He set off on the journey in agony. The longest journeys are the ones made in childhood. Now, the life he was leaving behind was another world, an irreversible one, and what appeared on the horizon were the clouds of a foreign sky.

"Grandpa," said Ferdy in his first letter, "I realized when I saw Istanbul that the most beautiful city is the city without war, but still, I miss you and smoke-coated Berlin." In response to this, his grandfather advised him not to neglect painting. "One begins to paint in order to forget, then one paints with the desire to remember." In his second letter Ferdy wrote that his headaches had become less frequent and he was beginning to get used to Istanbul. He said he was making friends with Jews, Christians, and Muslims, and his best friend was a girl whose father was Kurdish and mother was Armenian. He now saw that everyone had a different color and his grandfather's words about the race of people started to make sense to him.

He spoke with Amalya about this and told her a story he had heard from his grandfather. Once, a writer named Franz Kafka came across a little girl who was weeping in a park. The girl had lost her doll, and Franz said to her, "I am going to look for your doll now and meet you here tomorrow." The next day he brought a letter from the doll and read it to the girl. "Please, don't be sad. I have gone on a long journey to see the world myself. I will write to you often about what I have seen." Every day Franz brought the girl a new letter. After three weeks, he came with a doll. "Look," he said, "this is your baby doll, it returned to you." The girl was happy to have her doll back with her, but said the doll looked a bit different. Franz said, "Journeys always change people." Everybody had a journey like this in their lifetime. Ferdy spoke sadly. "As we were about to part, my grandfather told me this story. Now I understand him. The journey has changed me as well." The next day Amalya met him with a book in her hand. "There was a book by your Franz at our house. I found it among my uncle's books. But it's in German, I can't understand it." Ferdy took the book, he read the first story, translating it piece by piece. They read a story every

day. Sometimes they would laugh, and sometimes they would feel anxious. As they finished
the book, they said, "Our Franz." They repeated
it: "He is our Franz."

After Amalya moved to France, Ferdy Kaplan
faced the sorrow of discrimination on two more
occasions. During the pogrom on non-Muslims in
Istanbul in September 1955, which resulted in the
murder of 17 people, the rape of 60 women, and
the looting of 5,317 homes, shops, churches, and
synagogues, Ferdy's German identity was remembered too. He was beaten up in the neighborhood
square and his leg was broken. They all, including one of his friends from high school, made fun
of him. They wrote his name on the wall, spell-
ing it *Ferdi*. "Wasn't your father a Turk? Why do
you spell your name with a *y*, like Germans, but
not with an *i*, like Turks?" Ferdy stayed at home,
bedridden for weeks. The distress grew inside
him. One night he awoke from his sleep with a
start. He told his dream to his grandmother. "In
the dream, I saw my mother. We were in a city
I never knew, standing in an empty street. She
came and took me in her arms. Stay with me, she
said. I was still a child. I cried and said, Don't
leave me alone, Mommy." His grandmother told
him that this dream was a sign that he should go
back to Germany, where it would be safer for him
to live. Ferdy was determined that he would stay

in Istanbul and in his neighborhood. However, six months later, upon the passing of his grandmother, he moved to another neighborhood. As he was moving away, he did something that had long been on his mind. He followed his old friend from high school who was responsible for breaking his leg. Catching him in a dark corner, he hit him with a stick and broke his nose. Covering his face with a mask, Ferdy vanished into the narrow streets. Five years later, when Ferdy took part in anti-government protests, the images of those days were fresh in his mind. He was convinced that it was time for politics to change, for him and for everyone. He was arrested during a demonstration. The police made him remember his father, as did his old friends from the neighborhood. "Your father was a nationalist, why are you acting against your nation? Or is it German blood in your veins instead of Turkish blood?" Ferdy ignored these taunts, which he was used to. His mind was busy with Amalya. The same day she was leaving for Paris, but Ferdy wouldn't be able to see her off and say goodbye.

JUDGE: "Mr. Prosecutor, is there a link between this attack and the other attacks on the student leaders? Are you still considering this option?"

PROSECUTOR: "Your Honor, we are not certain, we are still looking into it. This may be part of their plan to cause chaos and instability in our country. If they succeed, they will present their antiquated ideas as a new hope."

JUDGE: "You need to find some factual evidence. Otherwise, the case will have no foundation."

PROSECUTOR: "Yes, I know. I am sure we will get some solid evidence soon."

FERDY KAPLAN: "I don't think that's possible."

PROSECUTOR: "Mr. Kaplan, you are persistently trying to show your self-confidence, but this confidence is groundless."

FERDY KAPLAN: "It's not as groundless as your claims, we know that."

PROSECUTOR: "You always state your disagreement, yet you do not provide us with any information."

FERDY KAPLAN: "Do I not provide you with information, indeed? You had no idea who the old man was, you realized his identity when I told you. What more do you want?"

PROSECUTOR: "We want to know what your purpose is. We want to know about your organization, your collaborators, and your new plans."

FERDY KAPLAN: "I'll tell you the same things, but again you won't understand me."

PROSECUTOR: "What are you going to tell us?"

FERDY KAPLAN: "You are searching in the wrong place. You are not even trying to look in the right place."

PROSECUTOR: "Where should we look, Mr. Kaplan? You wounded a writer and you killed a student. Where else should we look?"

FERDY KAPLAN: "It is as if I'm leading this hearing, not you! If I stop speaking, you will be stranded, marking time."

PROSECUTOR: "I don't think so at all. When you tried to run away at the scene, we apprehended you and brought you here. We found the Nazi roots in your past. We searched the connections of your parents. We obtained information about you from Istanbul. We put the case within a framework."

FERDY KAPLAN: "This framework is founded on nothing. If you could look at it from any distance, you would understand, but you prefer to believe in meaningless stories."

PROSECUTOR: "What is wrong with these stories? During the war you were in Berlin. You were taken by your family to Nazi rallies. You grew up with that enthusiasm and pride."

FERDY KAPLAN: "These are the parts of my life that have long been forgotten."

PROSECUTOR: "You may have forgotten, but you were reminded all your life in Istanbul. There you encountered hostility toward foreigners, you were assaulted, you were humiliated, and as a result, your faith was reawakened."

FERDY KAPLAN: "You are drawing the wrong conclusions from real events."

PROSECUTOR: "In my opinion, you took the wrong path due to certain events. Those events reconnected you with past memories, and now you have decided to create a future that your parents couldn't achieve."

FERDY KAPLAN: "That's enough—"

PROSECUTOR: "When you heard the truth—"

FERDY KAPLAN: "I have not heard a single true word from you. You are trying to put your lies in my mouth."

PROSECUTOR: "Why are you agitated?"

FERDY KAPLAN: "I defend the things I have done, but you are asking me to become someone I am not, you are forcing me to wear a straitjacket."

PROSECUTOR: "We are not forcing you to wear anything. I do not doubt your sanity. For now, however, you need to see the insanity of the crime you committed. You are trying to bring a dead idea and a dark history back to life."

FERDY KAPLAN: "The racism you are describing is nothing to me but a wound from my childhood."

PROSECUTOR: "What if that wound had been reopened?"

FERDY KAPLAN: "That wound was a big mistake, and it was buried under the rubble of history, along with my parents."

PROSECUTOR: "I want to believe what you say, but it doesn't seem to help us in explaining the chain of events."

FERDY KAPLAN: "Forget about the chain of events, let it go, just believe my words."

PROSECUTOR: "Why are you before this court, then? You tell us, go on. Why did you try to kill a Jewish writer?"

FERDY KAPLAN: "I did not try to kill a Jewish writer."

PROSECUTOR: "Oh, now, is this a new game you are going to play? It was only yesterday that you told us how you aimed to kill Max Brod."

FERDY KAPLAN: "A man is not just his identity."

PROSECUTOR: "Are you talking about his Jewishness?"

FERDY KAPLAN: "Well, I consider Max Brod not as a Jewish writer but as Franz Kafka's most trusted friend. That's how I see him."

JUDGE: "Mr. Kaplan, you will answer the prosecution's allegations more clearly. I don't understand what you are saying. If you aren't a racist, then what are you?"

FERDY KAPLAN: "What am I supposed to be?"

JUDGE: "I'm asking you, Mr. Kaplan. What are you?"

FERDY KAPLAN: "I'm just a volunteer trying to fulfill the wishes of a dead person."

JUDGE: "What wishes? What has that got to do with the attack?"

FERDY KAPLAN: "The event has nothing to do with race and religion, contrary to what you claim. I came here to kill a writer who became disloyal to his friend."

JUDGE: "You are saying Max Brod was disloyal. To whom?"

FERDY KAPLAN: "To Franz Kafka."

JUDGE: "Kafka?"

FERDY KAPLAN: "The word 'disloyal' is not enough. He betrayed him."

JUDGE: "Mr. Kaplan, explain that clearly."

FERDY KAPLAN: "When Kafka died, in his Will he asked Mr. Brod burn all his writings and manuscripts. He was not satisfied with just one, he left two separate handwritten wills, almost begging Mr. Brod."

JUDGE: "So you say this is not only disloyalty but betrayal—"

FERDY KAPLAN: "Mr. Brod ignored the wishes of his best friend, and instead of burning his manuscripts, he published them one by one."

4 WEST BERLIN PRISON

The police make inquiries in Paris and Tel Aviv and request new sets of documents. They look into the books of Max Brod and Franz Kafka. In a trial that is going in a direction they don't understand, they are searching for satisfactory data, as they want to put what the defendant says into a coherent framework.

Commissioner Müller goes to see Ferdy Kaplan in Tegel Prison. In the interview room, he places two cups of coffee on the table. He watches Ferdy Kaplan drink his coffee and occasionally turn his head to look out of the window at the courtyard.

FERDY KAPLAN: "Coffee is good for a headache."

COMMISSIONER MÜLLER: "Do you have a headache?"

FERDY KAPLAN: "Can I have a cigarette?"

COMMISSIONER MÜLLER: "Of course, here you are."

FERDY KAPLAN: "Thank you."

COMMISSIONER MÜLLER: "You look tired, Mr. Kaplan, are you not sleeping well?"

FERDY KAPLAN: "It's not possible to sleep. I keep thinking over the same things."

COMMISSIONER MÜLLER: "Now, that is difficult for me to understand. You openly defend the attack, even feeling proud of it, and then you can't sleep because of anxiety. Is that it?"

FERDY KAPLAN: "It's not anxiety, it is grief. My head is full of faces and voices. The face of the dead young man, the sound of his mother's cry…"

COMMISSIONER MÜLLER: "These are things that will always live with you."

FERDY KAPLAN: "And why are you so relieved? Is it because the case has been solved?"

COMMISSIONER MÜLLER: "The case hasn't been solved yet. We have only your words about the events that led to the trial, and yet there are a lot of unanswered questions."

FERDY KAPLAN: "Still, you seem relaxed."

COMMISSIONER MÜLLER: "Well, we are glad to hear that this attack was not motivated by anti-Semitism. This country is ready to face the death of great authors, but not the reopening of old wounds."

FERDY KAPLAN: "After hearing my words, the prosecutor and the judge sighed with relief. So, that is the reason—"

COMMISSIONER MÜLLER: "Sometimes it's not the crime itself that counts, but its objective."

FERDY KAPLAN: "In spite of this, the journalists will say that it all stems from anti-Jewish motives. It is a Jewish writer from Israel that we are talking about."

COMMISSIONER MÜLLER: "Frankly, Mr. Kaplan, we trust your testimony. If the incident leaks to the press and there appear any unwanted comments, then we will have to release your statements."

FERDY KAPLAN: "I didn't see any journalists at the hearings. Am I right?"

COMMISSIONER MÜLLER: "We are keeping the case away from the press. They seem to be satisfied with the story we put out initially, that the murder was fueled by jealousy. That is why we are now keeping the name of Max Brod concealed, which is also Mr. Brod's wish. He doesn't want to bother with the journalists."

FERDY KAPLAN: "So why are you here?"

COMMISSIONER MÜLLER: "We wanted to pay a private visit to you."

FERDY KAPLAN: "As far as I know, under the law, once the trial begins the police have no leading role in the case. Is that right?"

COMMISSIONER MÜLLER: "Well, we just wanted to make a visit off the record."

FERDY KAPLAN: "You are keeping me in this prison. Is that also off the record? Only those convicted stay here. Prisoners whose trials are ongoing, like mine, do not stay here. Why is that?"

COMMISSIONER MÜLLER: "It's a security measure. We have no knowledge of what kind of an organization is behind you and what they are capable of. We thought it would be better to keep you in a more secure place."

FERDY KAPLAN: "And is it another of your precautionary measures to have police escorts alongside the prison officers who take me from the prison to the courtroom? Is that the reason the police join them?"

COMMISSIONER MÜLLER: "Yes, that is the precise reason. We accompany you for security during your transfer."

FERDY KAPLAN: "You say that you defend the law against me, yet you are breaching the law at every turn."

COMMISSIONER MÜLLER: "If you had helped us, by being more cooperative, surely we would have acted differently."

FERDY KAPLAN: "You don't need to take such measures for me, Mr. Müller. I'm not such an important person."

COMMISSIONER MÜLLER: "If only I could believe you. We have information on your identity, Mr. Kaplan, but we don't know who you really are. We are trying to navigate our way in the dark."

FERDY KAPLAN: "Now you are here with the hope of broadening your horizons through this meeting. Is that so?"

COMMISSIONER MÜLLER: "I have a few questions to go through and evaluate with you, that's why I wanted to talk to you."

FERDY KAPLAN: "It's fine, that's no problem for me. I am listening to you."

COMMISSIONER MÜLLER: "We better speak freely. There is no need to record this conversation, so we are able to clarify any uncertain points. We need convincing information and to be clear of the motive.

And with any details that don't have to go into your official statement—"

FERDY KAPLAN: "And you expect me to cooperate with you?"

COMMISSIONER MÜLLER: "Do not misunderstand me, I don't want any names. I won't even ask you about the woman who was with you during the attack. You can keep that to yourself."

FERDY KAPLAN: "So what do you want?"

COMMISSIONER MÜLLER: "If you just point us in the right direction and stop us from going down the wrong path, that's enough."

FERDY KAPLAN: "The prosecutor refused to do that when I suggested it at the hearing."

COMMISSIONER MÜLLER: "I will not reject it. I am going to pay attention to the direction you take us."

FERDY KAPLAN: "Why should I do that?"

COMMISSIONER MÜLLER: "If you help us, then we will help you. We are going to make sure that you get a reduced sentence from the court."

FERDY KAPLAN: "I'm not that kind of person, and you should have realized that by now."

COMMISSIONER MÜLLER: "There is no doubt about it at all. You don't have to disclose anything, but what's the harm in a little talk? Look, we've already started. *(Commissioner Müller takes two cigarettes out of his pack and offers one to Ferdy Kaplan.)* Here, have another one."

FERDY KAPLAN: "You are very generous today."

COMMISSIONER MÜLLER: "If the reason for the incident is as you say, that is, if the attack was intended to punish Mr. Brod for disregarding Kafka's will and publishing his works, then the case may well be closed there. But, Mr. Kaplan, we really need to know whether there are plans to target other writers."

FERDY KAPLAN: "Is that your worry? There is no need for that. I'm only in pursuit of Mr. Brod."

COMMISSIONER MÜLLER: "What about the others? Are the others planning to harm any writers?"

FERDY KAPLAN: "What others?"

COMMISSIONER MÜLLER: "People around *Stylo Noir* magazine."

FERDY KAPLAN: "*Stylo Noir*?"

COMMISSIONER MÜLLER: "Yes."

FERDY KAPLAN: "You surprise me, Mr. Müller, for the first time! Have you been reading those magazines?"

COMMISSIONER MÜLLER: "Yes, I started reading them yesterday."

FERDY KAPLAN: "Do you know French?"

COMMISSIONER MÜLLER: "I lived in France when I was young. My wife is French."

FERDY KAPLAN: "Oh, is that so? Then please give my best regards to your wife."

COMMISSIONER MÜLLER: "We have found some new information. We know that the argument over Kafka began in *Stylo Noir*. We would like to discuss this with you and, how shall I put it, we would like to broaden our literary culture a little. *(Commissioner Müller laughs and the three police officers sitting at the next table join in.)* In fact, I know Kafka from the books my wife reads, but I have never heard of Max Brod. Now, thanks to you, I have read both Kafka and Brod. I understand that they were very close friends. Shall I tell you what I think right from the beginning?"

FERDY KAPLAN: "Yes, please."

COMMISSIONER MÜLLER: "I think Mr. Brod acted correctly. I personally did not expect Mr. Brod to agree just because Kafka wanted to burn all his works. A good friend is someone who, despite you, I mean despite your mistakes, does the right thing for you. If not, he is not a friend but a servant following in your suit."

FERDY KAPLAN: "Satan had the same opinion."

COMMISSIONER MÜLLER: "Satan?"

FERDY KAPLAN: "When God created man in his own image, Satan objected. His objection was that after the creation of humans there would be corruption of God's uniqueness and that God's inimitableness would be lost. Satan disobeyed God with the sole purpose of trying to protect God. It is like Mr. Brod disobeying Kafka in order to protect Kafka."

COMMISSIONER MÜLLER: "That's interesting."

FERDY KAPLAN: "People like him deserve Dante's *Inferno*."

COMMISSIONER MÜLLER: "That's even more interesting."

FERDY KAPLAN: "Are you going to keep repeating the same word... 'interesting, interesting'..."

COMMISSIONER MÜLLER: "You are comparing Mr. Brod to Satan, who disobeyed God. So you wish to obey God's will, or rather try to fulfill his will, by punishing Mr. Brod. Is that so?"

FERDY KAPLAN: "You may see it that way, if you like..."

(Commissioner Müller holds one of the magazines in front of him.)

COMMISSIONER MÜLLER: "I will use this word again and say that this coincidence is most interesting. I read an article last night in an old issue of *Stylo Noir*. It explores the idea that it is free will that brings man closer to God. Aha, here it is! 'Kafka's Wishes' is the title of the article. Or perhaps I should interpret it as 'Kafka's Will'? The author of the article uses a pen name, no doubt. By any chance, could you be the author, Mr. Kaplan?"

FERDY KAPLAN: "You've really done your homework, Mr. Müller, but I am not the author of that piece."

COMMISSIONER MÜLLER: "Look, they are the same words as yours that are written here. The words 'God,' 'Satan,' 'Kafka,' and 'Brod' are repeated over and over again. Even Dante is here."

FERDY KAPLAN: "I read that article when it was published. It did a good job of explaining the confusion between right and wrong. Satan falls into wrongdoing in his search to find the right thing to do."

COMMISSIONER MÜLLER: "Or, by going in the wrong direction, Satan ends up finding the right result."

FERDY KAPLAN: "One could think that way..."

COMMISSIONER MÜLLER: "Well, you know *Stylo Noir* means 'black pen,' so most of the writers here use pseudonyms to hide their identities in the dark shadow of their pens. The magazine attracted more attention with its Kafka debate than with its mysterious authors. *(Commissioner Müller takes a file out of his bag.)* Here, the French police sent us some photographs. They believe that some of them are possibly those writers in *Stylo Noir*. Have a look."

(Ferdy Kaplan glances at the photos.)

FERDY KAPLAN: "Well, my photo is not here."

COMMISSIONER MÜLLER: "Did you notice the photographs of women?"

FERDY KAPLAN: "No. Why?"

COMMISSIONER MÜLLER: "They all have short hair."

FERDY KAPLAN: "Do you think this has meaning?"

COMMISSIONER MÜLLER: "Yes, it has meaning, but it has nothing to do with the case."

FERDY KAPLAN: "Well, I wonder—"

COMMISSIONER MÜLLER: "You know the movie *Breathless—À bout de souffle*—don't you? Since that movie, French women have changed. The starring actress, Jean Seberg, inspired everyone to have their hair cut short like hers. Look, the women in these photographs are a reflection of her."

FERDY KAPLAN: "A strange assumption."

COMMISSIONER MÜLLER: "Our German women do not have such a movie. I mean they do not have an idol who can attract the attention of young people."

FERDY KAPLAN: "Maybe they have one, but men can't see it. No, I mean to say that the police can't see it."

(Ferdy Kaplan laughs for the first time.)

Amalya was heavyhearted when she returned to Paris. It's as if she couldn't hear her mother, and she was not aware of the presence of her mother's partner, Doctor Hugo. She stayed away from their conversations. In the evenings, she retreated to her room and ate meals alone. One day, when they went out to a movie on her mother's insistence, she said to her, "Eliz, when I wrote to you, I told you that if you wanted to die happy, you should never see the new face of Istanbul. Well, same for me, I will no longer see it again either. I will keep hold of the old Istanbul that I know and store its love in my heart."

Amalya opened her suitcase a few days later. She took out the picture Ferdy had drawn and hung it above her desk. Her mother and Doctor Hugo came in and looked at the picture. "Doctor," Amalya said, "you have good taste and a knowledge of art. Tell me what you think of this picture." Doctor Hugo approached. "I must say, I have never seen such pencil use nor perspective before. Who is the artist?" Amalya said,

"A friend of mine in Istanbul drew it." Doctor Hugo stepped back and looked from a distance. "This is a friend who views you and Istanbul in a unique way. The woman in the picture is clearly you, but he has drawn a look that I have never seen on your face before. It is impressive." "If you say so, then it must be right," said Amalya, fixing her eyes on the picture.

Amalya began to drink heavily to rid herself of the thoughts gathering in her head. She would hang around the dark streets in the heart of the Latin Quarter and come home late at night. Thinking it might do her good, Doctor Hugo introduced her to the young people who published *Stylo Noir*. The magazine was very popular with students. It published a survey on the question "Should Kafka be burned?" and that fired a debate in school canteens and dimly lit bars. The magazine announced the results of the survey on its center pages: "Kafka should be burned!" A letter to the magazine from a reader stated: "Kafka can no longer be erased, but Max Brod, who was unfaithful to him, may pay the price." Then the magazine asked its readers: "Should Max Brod pay the price?" Canteens and bars were stirred with more heated debates. The result of the survey appeared on the cover of the magazine, this time with a black-and-white photograph: "Max Brod must pay the price!"

Amalya took part in the debates, sold *Stylo Noir* in the canteens, stayed at the magazine's office overnight sometimes, but still couldn't manage to get Istanbul out of her mind. She wandered around like a drunk, even when she did not drink a single drop of anything. Eliz spoke about her with Doctor Hugo: "I have tried everything, there's nothing else I can do. You tell me, what I should do?" Doctor Hugo suggested that they all take a trip and go away from the city for a few days. "Where to?" Eliz asked. "We will go visit my village," Doctor Hugo said. They left Paris in the early hours the following morning and headed south. They drove for six hours, with stops for rest and refreshment, through the orange-shaded autumnal countryside. As soon as they reached the village of Oradour-sur-Glane, they checked into a hotel and went out to have a look around. Doctor Hugo told them that there was no one left of his family in the village and that this was the second time he had come here since the war. When he passed the church, he came across an old woman. He hugged the woman, said a few words to her, and left. "That woman was my mother's friend," he said. He looked at the surrounding buildings and colorful walls, rubbing his eyes. Eliz asked him, "Are you okay, my dear?" Doctor Hugo smiled and said, "You know, I was born in this village, but this is not the village where I was born." Eliz stared at him. "What does that mean? You are bringing us to your village and speaking in vague words. As if you are a stranger here, not us, and you are looking around, confused."

After strolling through a few streets, they crossed over to the other side of the main road. Doctor Hugo pointed to the ruins ahead: "There is the village where I was born." Amid the trees were abandoned old houses. Partially collapsed walls. Fragments of broken bricks. Burned cars. "During the war I was not in this area, but around Paris," he explained. "The Normandy landings had just begun. Attacks against the Nazis and their collaborators increased from all sides. Here the Resistance managed to capture an SS officer named Helmut Kämpfe. No ordinary officer, he was one of the few commanders to have worn the most important medals awarded by the Nazis, and he was a favorite of Hitler. Two people from the French militia gave the Germans intelligence that the officer was being held in the village of Oradour-sur-Glane. The intelligence was incorrect. The Resistance had killed Helmut Kämpfe as soon as they captured him and, without delay, they left the area. The forces of the 2nd SS Panzer Division Das Reich surrounded the village but could not find any trace of the officer, so they decided to punish the villagers.

It was the fifth day of the Normandy landings, and they were full of rage. They gathered up the women and children in the church. They locked the men in the few barns. First, they turned their machine guns on the barns. They shot the men in the legs and while the men were lying on the ground wounded, they poured petrol on them and set them on fire. Next, they went to the church. They placed explosives by the wall, causing panic. As the women and children threw themselves at the doors and windows, trying to escape but unable to, they were met with the merciless sound of machine guns. That night, the Nazi army looted and burned all the houses. I have memorized the numbers: 247 women, 205 children, and 190 men were killed. Among those were my mother, my father, and my sister. When the war ended, it was decided to leave the village as it was and build a new one on the other side of the road. I came to help with the construction of the new village, worked for a few months, and then left. This is the first time I've been back since then."

Doctor Hugo showed them the corner covered with grass and rocks where his family's house had once stood. He walked slowly alongside the cemetery, without speaking. After that he turned back to the new village. With Eliz on one side and Amalya on the other, he walked up and down the streets of the new village until the sky grew dark. A few times he greeted the people he knew and told Eliz and Amalya their stories. "Those responsible," said Doctor Hugo, "they were all punished for their deeds, not only the Germans but their French collaborators too. The French militia leader Joseph Darnand, a brutal murderer, was captured in Italy after escaping, tried, and executed by firing squad. So one of the two militiamen who targeted this village was captured and executed. But there is also one militia man left who, for years, has not yet been nailed. My friends from the old Resistance group are following his trail. They recently discovered that he is living in Paris under a false identity. It is just a matter of time; he will be apprehended before long."

They had dinner at the restaurant next to the hotel. Eliz held Doctor Hugo's hand. "Now I understand why you never wanted to talk about your past. I wish you had brought us here earlier," she said. "You are right," he said, "I brought you here with the hope that Amalya would breathe the fresh air of a different environment, but this trip has been good for me too. Not only the faces of my loved ones but those ruined houses and graves have also lived within my mind for years, they come with me everywhere." Amalya took Doctor Hugo's hand too. "I know you take care of me, thank you very much. I want you to not worry about me anymore, Doctor Hugo, I'll be better from now on."

COMMISSIONER MÜLLER: "Would you have wanted to meet Mr. Brod?"

FERDY KAPLAN: "You can't imagine how much I wanted to meet him."

COMMISSIONER MÜLLER: "Then, this is news for you. Mr. Brod will be attending the hearing."

FERDY KAPLAN: "Now, this news is something to be happy about. There are matters I want to discuss with him. And I'll get a chance to tell him how much I love his books."

COMMISSIONER MÜLLER: "Love them?"

FERDY KAPLAN: "Don't think that I despise him. I esteem him and I admire his literature. In religious beliefs, you know, there are lists of 'Deadly Sins.' If there were such 'Deadly Sins' in literature, more's the pity, Mr. Brod has committed one of them. He crushed the soul of a fellow writer by disrespecting his will."

COMMISSIONER MÜLLER: "I can't understand you, no matter how hard I try."

FERDY KAPLAN: "Let me explain it this way. If Kafka were alive today, what would he do? He would burn all his manuscripts and continue to love his friend, Brod. I too love Brod, but at the same time I defend the right of Franz Kafka's will."

COMMISSIONER MÜLLER: "You mentioned a list of 'Deadly Sins' in literature. Who else do you have on that list?"

FERDY KAPLAN: "Mine is a one-man list, there is nobody else, I assure you."

COMMISSIONER MÜLLER: "I find it a little hard to believe you, Mr. Kaplan. Although your words and your tone are very convincing, these old issues of *Stylo Noir* still confuse me. Look, one issue three years ago praises the Watts Riots of the Black community in Los Angeles."

FERDY KAPLAN: "The people wanted their rights against inequality, they wanted an end to racist oppression, what's wrong with that?"

COMMISSIONER MÜLLER: "Is this the way to protect rights? More than thirty people died."

FERDY KAPLAN: "You know that it was the police who killed all of them. It's amazing how a Berlin police officer is defending the Los Angeles police. Is that what you call police solidarity?"

COMMISSIONER MÜLLER: "I don't defend the police there. I say riots and violence are the wrong way."

FERDY KAPLAN: "Who caused that to happen? Those who died there were innocent. And tell me, what does this have to do with me?"

COMMISSIONER MÜLLER: "When I see that death is easily justified, I become suspicious. You divide the dead into innocent and guilty. In this way you rationalize killing and coolly go after an old man like Max Brod."

FERDY KAPLAN: "Ah, Commissioner Müller, are you aware where we are now? This is a prison and its history is full of the brutality of the state against people, and that brutality is not limited to the Nazi era. And you, as a public servant, are talking to me about the death of innocent people. If you smell these walls, try once, you will smell the rotting lives of the innocent people."

COMMISSIONER MÜLLER: "There is some truth in what you say, I cannot deny that. But we both know that you are not one of those innocent people you are speaking of."

FERDY KAPLAN: "Don't worry about me, that is not important. Tell me about Mr. Brod. He must be feeling well, since he is able to attend the hearing."

COMMISSIONER MÜLLER: "Yes, I saw him yesterday. His wound's not terribly disturbing. He was shot in the shoulder. The doctors said he would lead a comfortable normal life again."

FERDY KAPLAN: "Good news."

COMMISSIONER MÜLLER: "Good news? Are you sure about that?"

FERDY KAPLAN: "I don't think you'll understand, even if I try to explain."

COMMISSIONER MÜLLER: "Had you seen Mr. Brod before, I mean before the day of the attack?"

FERDY KAPLAN: "No."

COMMISSIONER MÜLLER: "Mr. Brod said he could attend the hearing with his assistant. He turned down the offer of a police escort. He is a brave man. I will send a team to accompany him anyway. I don't want anything unfortunate to happen to him again. You know, the woman with the short hair is still free, wandering around."

FERDY KAPLAN: "Don't worry, nothing more will happen to Mr. Brod. Some traditions are sacred. In the past, when a man was being hanged, if the rope broke, it was regarded as though the sun of life had smiled upon him, and he would be pardoned. I hold to this tradition. Mr. Brod's rope broke and now he is free."

COMMISSIONER MÜLLER: "The writings in *Stylo Noir* are full of such weird references. Ancient times, traditions, revolutions, religions, retributions... It's impossible to say whether the publishers of this magazine are anarchists, communists, nihilists, or simply lunatics—"

FERDY KAPLAN: "They are not lunatics, that is for certain. I can only tell you this."

COMMISSIONER MÜLLER: "If only I could believe you, Mr. Kaplan."

FERDY KAPLAN: "Believe me, Mr. Müller."

COMMISSIONER MÜLLER: "And there is something else. Something that you and I have in common."

FERDY KAPLAN: "What is that?"

COMMISSIONER MÜLLER: "The women you and I love both have the same hairstyle. My wife used to have long hair, but like all French women, she now cuts it short."

FERDY KAPLAN: "Do you like it that way?"

COMMISSIONER MÜLLER: "Yes, I like it. And you?"

FERDY KAPLAN: "Mr. Müller, I think I made a mistake at the outset and underestimated your intelligence."

5 WEST BERLIN COURTROOM

Max Brod leaves Berlin without informing the authorities of his departure. In a letter to the court, he apologizes for not attending the hearing:

"I am an old man. All this whirl is too much for me. I am going back home. My home is also Kafka's home. He and I, we completed each other. He feared death because he could not live as he pleased. And so I lived this life in his stead too. Kafka left me two notes asking that all his works be burned. He had always shied away from publishing his work. One or two of his works were published following my encouragement. His will was like that of a lover who is going away and saying Forget me, and yet he has no desire to be forgotten ever. I knew it.

At the beginning I felt eternal happiness at having published Kafka's works, so they saw the light of day. As I grew older, the joy in my heart started to dull and be replaced by a sense of unhappiness. I began to liken myself to Satan. Satan, who disobeyed God with the pure intention of defending God. Kafka was my God and I had disregarded his will. If Dante were alive today, he would have found me deserving of the *Inferno* in his *Comedy*." (While this part of the letter is being read, Ferdy Kaplan turns and looks at Commissioner Müller, who is sitting in the row to his right. Commissioner Müller likewise turns his head toward Ferdy Kaplan.) "Your Honor, had I come to court and been present, I would not have been able to assist you. I did not see the attackers. I cannot identify them. Whoever they are, I forgive them. I only wish that they had been a little more careful and sent an old man like me to the other world instead of some innocent young student. That would have pleased me."

PROSECUTOR: "Mr. Kaplan, did you intend to murder this kind of man?"

FERDY KAPLAN: "Well, to be honest, I hadn't even considered the idea that Mr. Brod might feel the slightest remorse toward Kafka."

PROSECUTOR: "He is a man who has done good both to Kafka and to literature itself."

FERDY KAPLAN: "I wouldn't go that far."

PROSECUTOR: "Why?"

FERDY KAPLAN: "Mr. Brod published those manuscripts in his possession by altering and editing them. It is not known where he found the authority and right to do this. Publishing a text by altering it means ruining it."

PROSECUTOR: "On what basis do you say this?"

FERDY KAPLAN: "Let me give you an example. Kafka wrote a novel by the name *The Man Who Disappeared*. Mr. Brod published it under the title *Amerika*. Even the title was changed, so how can we really know how much of the content of this book belongs to Kafka?"

PROSECUTOR: "Perhaps that was an appropriate change to make."

FERDY KAPLAN: "Is it appropriate for Kafka or for Brod? For instance, Kafka liked long paragraphs, yet

Brod cut them up and separated the lines. To whom is this appropriate?"

PROSECUTOR: "I just said that as a generalization. I cannot comment much as I haven't read the book."

FERDY KAPLAN: "Have you read any Kafka?"

PROSECUTOR: "In fact, I have read only one of his books. Now, due to the developments in this case, I have bought some of his books and hope to read them."

FERDY KAPLAN: "Which book did you read?"

PROSECUTOR: "*The Metamorphosis*. You know, a man who transforms into an insect."

FERDY KAPLAN: "Do you remember the cover of the book? What was the picture on it?"

PROSECUTOR: "I think... there was a gloomy-looking room... a huge insect hidden under the bed, well, the cover was like the story itself."

FERDY KAPLAN: "There it is, poor Kafka. He knew from the very outset that his books were going to be treated unfairly. He anticipated it. He himself sent *The Metamorphosis* to the publisher. Then he wrote a letter to the publisher, requesting them not to put a picture of an insect on the cover. He stressed that no insect should appear on the cover, not even in the background. The first publisher followed Kafka's request, but then what has happened after that? Fifty years have gone by and now, if you look at any cover, printed anywhere in the world, it is almost impossible to find one without an insect. Is that any way to understand and be loyal to Kafka?"

PROSECUTOR: "You are exaggerating, Mr. Kaplan. Regardless of the comments and the opinions, the readers understand these books and they pour their own feelings into the stories."

FERDY KAPLAN: "What Kafka left behind were the writings he kept for himself. Perhaps none of them were yet maturely formed, perhaps he would have changed them, make some longer, some shorter. Maybe Kafka was still working on those changes, struggling with them."

PROSECUTOR: "Whether they were missing something or were rough drafts, why should it be bad to read these texts after the death of the author and accept them in the state they were left?"

FERDY KAPLAN: "If the author had not expressed his desires, then what you say would make sense. But Kafka made his wishes clear before he died and did so in a certain way."

PROSECUTOR: "Even if we, just for the sake of argument, accept your point of view, it still does not justify your intention to kill. Just because someone has erred. Let's assume Max Brod was wrong in what he did, it doesn't mean that he deserved to die."

FERDY KAPLAN: "Mr. Prosecutor, in my opinion we are indebted to Kafka. I believe in the eternity of the human soul and in a person's free will. If someone disregards this eternity that is Kafka's will, then he should bear the punishment. Well, having seen the letter that he sent to the court, it is clear that Mr. Brod himself expected this punishment too."

PROSECUTOR: "If Kafka has any recognition as an important person, it is because of his writings. His name wouldn't mean anything had he written nothing. All this was made possible by Max Brod. Thanks to Brod, we know of the man Kafka. Why should we send Kafka to the realm of absence and nothingness, while he has already reached the realm of eternity through his writings?"

FERDY KAPLAN: "No matter how much Brod played with his works, he couldn't spoil the magic of Kafka's pen. Because Kafka had power. If there is such a person as Kafka today, it is not due to Max Brod but in spite of him."

PROSECUTOR: "If Kafka truly wanted his works to be burned, why didn't he burn them himself? He wrote continuously for many years, gathering his body of work, and did not attempt to destroy a single piece."

FERDY KAPLAN: "We don't know this for sure. Perhaps his works weren't yet complete. Perhaps he wanted them to be published under his own eyes. During the deteriorating course of his illness he realized that this would not be possible, yet he did not have the strength to destroy his own works. And so he left himself in the hands of his most trusted friend."

PROSECUTOR: "These are all speculations. No judgment can be made based upon this, and even if one could, it does not mean pursuing and murdering people. There is another way, which is to criticize people. I believe there have been people in the literary world who have written about Mr. Brod and criticized him, isn't that right?"

FERDY KAPLAN: "You're right, I've read many such criticisms."

PROSECUTOR: "If only you had been satisfied with criticism too."

FERDY KAPLAN: "You see Kafka as a literary treasure, and you are content to value this treasure, just like everybody else. But Kafka himself, as he approached the end of his life, no longer desired to identify himself as a writer. He was just a person, and that was all. I respect that person and his right to anonymity; I respect his choice to leave this world as he wished. That is what Mr. Brod ignored."

PROSECUTOR: "A person nearing death is like an insensible child. A child will want to touch the fire, so we intervene to prevent it. If a person who is about to die wants to throw his books into the fire, we shall step in to prevent him."

FERDY KAPLAN: "What is the right thing to do? Who decides that?"

PROSECUTOR: "There are very faithful readers of Kafka, let's leave it to them. They will protect Kafka."

FERDY KAPLAN: "Protect? He had three sisters, all of them were killed in the concentration camps. Who protected them?"

PROSECUTOR: "That's another question."

FERDY KAPLAN: "No, this is the real question. Had Kafka lived a little longer, he would have found himself in a concentration camp. Nobody would have protected him, just as there is nobody to protect him today."

PROSECUTOR: "History, our history, is full of mistakes. To avoid these mistakes recurring, we are in defense of justice, and we are defending Kafka here."

FERDY KAPLAN: "If you were committed to defending justice itself, you would not be sitting behind that desk but would be here, in my place. No, you are not on Kafka's side but, rather, on the side of his books. Just like Max Brod. Brod quickly forgot Kafka and only loved his written works. As he grew older, only then did he realize his mistake. When his love for Kafka as a person was rekindled years later, he felt that his deeds were those of a devil. He then felt remorseful. Did you know that Brod was also once an accomplished musician? He composed music and sang opera. In recent years, he returned to his love of music and distanced himself from literature. Although the remorse in his soul led him back toward music, he could not find peace of mind. He longed for death."

PROSECUTOR: "This is your interpretation, Mr. Kaplan. You are presenting your interpretation as if it were the wish of Max Brod."

FERDY KAPLAN: "Do you know how Kafka died? On his last night, he was in agony in a sanatorium. He asked the doctor there to put an end to his life. When the doctor refused, Kafka screamed, 'Kill me! If you don't kill me, you are a murderer.' And now Max Brod's soul is in agony, and he wants us to kill him. If we don't follow his request and kill him, then we are considered murderers. This is evident from what he wrote. His letter is short but perfectly clear."

PROSECUTOR: "You're drawing long conclusions from a short letter."

FERDY KAPLAN: "Mr. Prosecutor, I believe in the power of drawing long conclusions from short letters."

PROSECUTOR: "Again, more obscure words that are difficult to understand."

FERDY KAPLAN: "The distance between your chair and mine is so great that it's really hard for us to understand each other."

"Dear Amalya, I am writing you this postcard with a delay of six months and one week. Had I written any earlier, I would not have been able to say the words I want to say here. I couldn't come to the airport to say goodbye to you because I was under arrest. In custody, my German identity proved both a reason for my humiliation by the police and also an advantage. The others arrested with me at the protest stayed in custody for a week, but the police were not happy to see the German passport in my pocket, so they released me after two days. How could I write to you then? Even if I loved you, I had to hide it from you and from myself. Otherwise, I would have been unfair to my fiancée and disloyal to the life we'd dreamed of together. So I believed in time and thought I could bear your absence, but eventually, I was defeated by time. Last week, without realizing it, I called my fiancée by your name. Who is Amalya? she asked. What do you mean? I responded. You just called me Amalya, she said. Really? Yes, really. After six months, I fell into helplessness. I told her everything. We bowed our heads. We said farewell and separated. I've been wandering around for a week, and I don't know what to do. And now, on the back of a postcard on which I've drawn a view of Istanbul, I'm writing to tell you that I love you. Amalya! I believe in myself, in you, and in time."

It was a postcard covered in fine sketches that showed the viewpoint of a seagull as it flew over the Maiden's Tower and, behind it, the Bosphorus stretching out like a snake. The seagull was hanging with its wings open, suspended by the northeast wind. Amalya felt as though she were floating alongside the seagull, looking down and watching the people strolling on the shore. A ferry was crossing the Bosphorus, breaking waves one after the other. Amalya followed the ferry, dived into the wind, and descended to the rear deck, where she found Ferdy watching the sea. The sun was setting over Istanbul.

Amalya leaned toward Ferdy, over his mouth, and she inhaled his breath with a feeling of melancholy on the blowing wind. At that moment, her mother entered the room. Amalya placed the card on the table and turned to her mother. She told her about the beauty of old times and about how she missed Istanbul. "Is it only Istanbul that you miss?" asked her mother. "No, it's more," replied Amalya. "Go then, my dear, go and finish what you have left to do." Amalya smiled like a mischievous child and said, "I have a better idea."

PROSECUTOR: "Your Honor! The argument of defending Kafka's last will, and what's more, taking his revenge, was not the personal idea of the defendant. As we have established, this topic has been a matter of discussion in magazines in France for some twenty years."

JUDGE: "How? Were they openly speaking of revenge?"

PROSECUTOR: "Articles with such discourse were published, yes."

JUDGE: "I assume that you have some evidence to present."

PROSECUTOR: "We have some publications at hand. The issue was raised in *Axiome*, a magazine that ceased publication twenty years ago. Recently, *Stylo Noir*, a magazine popular among young people, has been covering this topic more frequently and in a sharper way."

JUDGE: "What sort of magazines are they? Are they publications of underground groups?"

PROSECUTOR: "*Axiome* was an underground publication by the French Resistance during the Second World War. In the years after the war, the magazine was published publicly and was in circulation until 1948.

In several issues they published debates on the topic 'Should Kafka be burned?' and ran a survey on this."

FERDY KAPLAN: "Mr. Prosecutor, are you trying to tell me about a debate that took place when I was a child?"

PROSECUTOR: "We're trying to get to the bottom of the idea to which you are bound and to ferret out the roots of the organization you are involved with."

JUDGE: "Mr. Kaplan, you can speak when it's your turn, but for the moment you must remain silent."

FERDY KAPLAN: "Well, I'm listening, let's see where you are heading."

JUDGE: "Mr. Prosecutor, you say that *Axiome* was published by the Resistance. While there were political issues to be engaged in during the war, why should they turn their attention to discussions of literary matters?"

PROSECUTOR: "From the very beginning, the magazine adopted subjects on art and culture. By weaving a thread of resistance through this field, it was able to maintain its political affiliations too."

JUDGE: "It would seem from your comments that *Axiome* magazine encouraged violence against certain writers. Is that so?"

PROSECUTOR: "I would say that applies more to *Stylo Noir*."

JUDGE: "Who publishes this magazine? The same people from the Resistance?"

PROSECUTOR: "No. A group of young people studying at different universities began publishing *Stylo Noir* ten years ago. It constantly renews itself with new contributors."

JUDGE: "Are these young people following in the footsteps of the previous generation?"

PROSECUTOR: "It seems that *Stylo Noir* inherited the idea of defending Kafka and his will from *Axiome*. Of course, they went further and gave way to the call to punish Max Brod."

JUDGE: "By 'punish,' what do they mean? Do they mean murder?"

PROSECUTOR: "They don't say it so clearly as that. They say that Max Brod should pay the price, they publish writings about that, but they don't specify what they mean by paying the price."

JUDGE: "It's a flexible expression, which can be taken in any direction."

PROSECUTOR: "Despite the ambiguity of the word 'price,' some expressions in the articles draw attention to a certain direction. I will mention some descriptive words they used in attributing Mr. Brod. *(The prosecutor holds up a paper and reads.)* 'Unfaithful' is what they call him, 'vile' and 'wretched.' They say he is more treacherous than the traitors during the war."

JUDGE: "Those are dangerous words. We know that traitors during the war were sentenced to death."

PROSECUTOR: "These kinds of articles and letters were published in the magazine."

JUDGE: "Well, did none of this arouse the attention of the authorities?"

PROSECUTOR: "*Stylo Noir* is the kind of magazine that adopts a satirical language, printing caricatures and often being humorous about serious subjects. Because it wasn't clear when they were being serious and when they were humorous, they didn't attract attention."

JUDGE: "Is it possible that the former publishers of *Axiome* strengthened a tie with the young people publishing *Stylo Noir* and led them in a certain direction?"

PROSECUTOR: "These are people from whom anything may be expected. For instance, one of the *Axiome* group appeared somewhere else. Seven years ago, a plane was hijacked in Portugal, and as it flew over Lisbon anti-government flyers were dropped all over the city. The hijackers then landed the plane in Morocco. One of those hijackers was a Resistance fighter who had published *Axiome*. We believe that these people have established a way of influencing the editorial staff of *Stylo Noir*."

JUDGE: "Very well. What is the nature of Ferdy Kaplan's affiliation with *Stylo Noir*?"

PROSECUTOR: "We are awaiting a new intelligence report from France. The defendant is not cooperating with us."

FERDY KAPLAN: "Your Honor, I have given both the prosecutor and the police very clear answers on this matter. *Stylo Noir* is a magazine that's available all over Paris. I buy it and read it like a lot of other people. I have no other affiliation with the magazine."

JUDGE: "Where did this idea come from, the idea for the attack on Max Brod and taking Kafka's revenge? Is it something you decided for yourself?"

FERDY KAPLAN: "Yes. I've been a fervent reader of Kafka for a number of years. Beyond his writings, I love and respect him as a person. Well, I'm mature enough to make my own decisions. I was not in need of anyone's order to carry out this mission."

JUDGE: "You shoot people and furthermore you brag about it, like this."

PROSECUTOR: "Your Honor, the defendant has a habit of speaking in an uncanny way. Even when he sometimes gives us useful information, he still prevents us from reaching any actual conclusion. He painted a picture for us, gave us a frame, but never mentioned what's behind it. For this reason, maybe the French magazines are an instrument to manipulate us. Perhaps there is another network here, like the involvement of a foreign intelligence service."

JUDGE: "Are you referring to East Germany? Are you still considering that as an option?"

PROSECUTOR: "The murder of a Jewish writer in the West could serve the interest of East Germany, as it would put the burden of the past back on this side. We are investigating this."

FERDY KAPLAN: "It is a waste of time, Mr. Prosecutor, it really is."

PROSECUTOR: "When you insist like this, we feel suspicious and prefer to envisage the opposite of what you indicate."

FERDY KAPLAN: "You've doubted everything I've said right from the beginning, and you have portrayed me by using all sorts of names. You have called me an anarchist, you have called me a lunatic. And now you are adding the title of a spy for East Germany. What kind of list is this?"

PROSECUTOR: "Mr. Kaplan, there is something else I would like to ask you. If you had succeeded in killing

Mr. Brod, would you have then moved on to another target? What would you have done next?"

FERDY KAPLAN: "I know exactly what I would have done. I would have written a letter to Mr. Brod. You may wonder what use it would be to write a letter to a dead man. Well, Kafka wrote a letter to his living father, he poured his heart into the pages, but he never gave the letter to his father. This tells us more than anything about the nature of Kafka's soul. Not every piece of writing is meant for publication. Kafka shared that letter with his mother and sisters but never with whom it had been addressed to: his father. He wrote the letter primarily for himself, for his past, for his weaknesses, and for his disappointments. And what happened upon Kafka's death? The forty-five-page letter he wrote to his father was turned into a book and published along with his other works all around the world under the title *Letter to His Father*. This is what hurts the human soul."

6 WEST BERLIN PRISON

The next morning Commissioner Müller comes to the prison, just as the first sunbeams fall on the windows. He and Ferdy Kaplan are sitting at the same table, facing each other. The chirps of birds outside can be heard. When the birds stop chirping, the room falls silent. They sip their coffee. With tired eyes they look at each other.

COMMISSIONER MÜLLER: "Still having difficulty sleeping, Mr. Kaplan? You look tired."

FERDY KAPLAN: "I see that you didn't manage to have a good sleep either."

(Ferdy Kaplan looks at Commissioner Müller and then at the police officers standing beside him.)

COMMISSIONER MÜLLER: "We are dealing with matters that keep us from sleeping. We spent the night on our feet. You could have slept. I would think that you'd be accustomed to living here."

FERDY KAPLAN: "Well, I am settling in, don't worry. Were you on the trail of new evidence?"

COMMISSIONER MÜLLER: "You know, we are running after constantly changing things."

FERDY KAPLAN: "Well, then, what are you here for at this time of the morning?"

COMMISSIONER MÜLLER: "You have a hearing, Mr. Kaplan, or did you forget about it? We are here to take you to the courthouse."

FERDY KAPLAN: "I asked what made you come here so early. The hearing is in the afternoon, yet you are here at the break of day. Or would you like to have another conversation with me off the record?"

COMMISSIONER MÜLLER: "This is what we need."

FERDY KAPLAN: "Did you start to feel confused again?"

COMMISSIONER MÜLLER: "Well, the threads in my mind have become a little tangled, and so I came to look for some solutions—with your help."

FERDY KAPLAN: "I hope you're not going to ask me the same old questions."

COMMISSIONER MÜLLER: "Not old ones, I have new questions."

FERDY KAPLAN: "New reports—"

COMMISSIONER MÜLLER: "No new reports at all. It was during the hearing yesterday that I lost my grip on the threads and felt like I was in a daze."

FERDY KAPLAN: "About what? There were many things discussed yesterday."

COMMISSIONER MÜLLER: "About the things Mr. Brod said in his letter—"

FERDY KAPLAN: "Oh, I see, God and Satan, and so on...Is that what you mean?"

COMMISSIONER MÜLLER: "Yes, those words...When the letter was being read, I noticed that you were surprised too."

FERDY KAPLAN: "How would it be possible not to be surprised? Those were phrases that I used when talking with you. For a moment I thought that this letter was fictitious, that you had written those words."

COMMISSIONER MÜLLER: "Are you serious? The tiredness on your face conceals your expression, Mr. Kaplan. I don't understand you."

FERDY KAPLAN: "It was just a momentary thought. I saw that it was not really a probability and so I wiped it from my mind."

COMMISSIONER MÜLLER: "I had no knowledge of that letter, I only learned of it at the same time as you, at the hearing."

FERDY KAPLAN: "Well, what did you think when you heard those words?"

COMMISSIONER MÜLLER: "Because I was so surprised, at first I couldn't think of anything."

FERDY KAPLAN: "I think Mr. Brod and I were subscribers to the same magazine. It seems that he too was following *Stylo Noir* and was reading articles about himself and Kafka."

COMMISSIONER MÜLLER: "Yes, that could be a possibility."

FERDY KAPLAN: "I knew that *Stylo Noir* was a much-read magazine in France, but I wasn't aware that its popularity had spread as far as Israel."

COMMISSIONER MÜLLER: "Mr. Kaplan, as you are speaking like this, I'd like to believe that you're just a reader of the magazine and you do not have any direct link to it."

FERDY KAPLAN: "So you should believe it then."

COMMISSIONER MÜLLER: "When you were listening to Mr. Brod's words, did any other possibility appear in your mind?"

FERDY KAPLAN: "Mr. Brod must have been smitten with that article in the magazine, and he had words such as 'God,' 'Satan,' and 'willpower' etched upon his mind. Just as I did. What else could it possibly be?"

COMMISSIONER MÜLLER: "Since you thought perhaps I had written Mr. Brod's letter, well, I could have had the same thought about you."

FERDY KAPLAN: "You mean me writing that letter? How would it be possible for me to do it from here?"

COMMISSIONER MÜLLER: "I know that it wouldn't have been possible. That's why I too wiped it from my mind and was left with only one possibility."

FERDY KAPLAN: "What possibility?"

COMMISSIONER MÜLLER: "It is about the true identity of the person who wrote the text."

FERDY KAPLAN: "You mean the article in the magazine?"

COMMISSIONER MÜLLER: "Yes."

FERDY KAPLAN: "Who wrote it? Actually, more to the point, what significance does it have here?"

COMMISSIONER MÜLLER: "It was of no significance before, but now it has become very significant."

FERDY KAPLAN: "Why?"

COMMISSIONER MÜLLER: "Let me ask you a question, so you can contemplate and weigh it, as I have been doing all night long."

FERDY KAPLAN: "Well, I feel curious about your question."

COMMISSIONER MÜLLER: "Mr. Kaplan, would you think that Max Brod himself wrote that article in the magazine? What would you say?"

FERDY KAPLAN: "Mr. Müller, are you trying to test me?"

COMMISSIONER MÜLLER: "Don't disregard it straightaway, think about it for a while and let its validity settle."

FERDY KAPLAN: "I can't read your expression due to the tiredness on your face. Are you serious?"

COMMISSIONER MÜLLER: "In my opinion, Mr. Brod's letter harbors a lot more signs than we first thought."

FERDY KAPLAN: "You are serious."

COMMISSIONER MÜLLER: "The articles in *Stylo Noir* were written under pseudonyms, so why shouldn't Max Brod be the author of one of them?"

FERDY KAPLAN: "I see, your point is that Mr. Brod wrote articles to stigmatize himself. That doesn't seem to me to be a very coherent argument."

COMMISSIONER MÜLLER: "Why? Didn't Mr. Brod do the same thing yesterday? In the letter he used critical words to describe himself and expressed his remorse."

FERDY KAPLAN: "I found his letter to be very sincere."

COMMISSIONER MÜLLER: "It is sincere, yes, that's why it reveals the truth."

FERDY KAPLAN: "But the article in the magazine was not just limited to criticism, it also mentioned paying the price. In your opinion, Mr. Brod wrote to the magazine promoting the idea that he should be punished for his actions. Is my understanding correct?"

COMMISSIONER MÜLLER: "Yes."

FERDY KAPLAN: "How strange."

(Ferdy Kaplan closes his eyes and lowers his head. He places his hand on his right temple.)

COMMISSIONER MÜLLER: "What's wrong, do you feel confused or upset?"

FERDY KAPLAN: "I have a headache. That's all."

COMMISSIONER MÜLLER: "Is that really all?"

FERDY KAPLAN: "Yes, it's a headache."

After several sleepless nights in front of the post-card of Istanbul, Amalya sat down at her desk. She wrote a long letter to Ferdy and said, "I don't know how to write briefly." She invited him to Paris and attached a poem to the end of her letter. *"You are Fate / You came from far away / Riding the horse of time / So far away once again / Come, that I may know / You are Fate."* While she was waiting for Ferdy, Amalya cut her hair. She rearranged her room. She bought a drawing table for Ferdy and placed paints, brushes, and pens on it. She went to the airport and upon seeing Ferdy, she gave him a big hug and kept him in her arms for a very long time. Then she asked him the question that she had not asked in Istanbul. "Are you still having headaches?" Ferdy replied, with surprise in his voice, "Not so often as before. Now and again." Amalya touched Ferdy's right temple, then reached out and kissed him on the lips. Together they joined the youths of Paris. They roamed around nightclubs filled with cigarette smoke and lively conversation, and this time, they read Kafka's books in French.

Ferdy drew a portrait of Kafka with a black pen and hung it on the wall. On the picture, he wrote: "Franz K." When Doctor Hugo came to their room the next day, he asked Ferdy why he had written Kafka's name in that way. "In the will that he left behind," Ferdy explained, "he made it clear that he didn't want to be known as 'the author Kafka' anymore. You know, in some novels he used only the initial K. as the name of the protagonist. It was the *K* for Kafka and it was a mirror of his own self that he never revealed. During our years in Istanbul, Amalya and I called him Franz and loved him by that name. Now we feel that this bears meaning. Calling him by his first name is respecting his right to be known as himself. For us, he is not the author Kafka but any other world citizen called Franz, he is Franz K."

Having taken a pen, Doctor Hugo approached the picture and added the words "Lovers of." The caption on the picture was altered to "Lovers of Franz K." Ferdy looked at Amalya with a smile. Then he asked Doctor Hugo about the debate brewing in *Stylo Noir* and wanted to know his thoughts on Max Brod. "I believe in the arguments developed by the philosopher Immanuel Kant," said Doctor Hugo. "In an article he wrote, Kant explains that even a person being chased by a lunatic murderer and whose life is in imminent danger must not tell a lie. Lies protect no one for good, the truth will always come out." Then

Doctor Hugo went on to tell them about the life of the poet Louis Aragon. Aragon was born in Paris and lived with his mother and grandmother, but he knew them as his elder sister and his foster mother. He thought that his father, who visited them occasionally, was his godfather. His father was married to someone else and so he refused to marry Aragon's mother and be a father to him. When Aragon was nineteen and about to join the army during the First World War, they told him the truth. Your sister is your mother, they said, your foster mother is your grandmother, and your godfather is actually your father. It was a time when those who went to war were not expected to return, and so as they were sending him into the arms of death, they revealed the truth to him. For Kant, truth was above everything else: above fear, love, even above death. The Aragon family acted accordingly as the breath of death came closer to them. "In my opinion," Doctor Hugo carried on, "Max Brod didn't remain loyal to the truth. He took no notice of human nature and ignored the wishes of his friend. It is a responsibility of life to stay faithful to the truth. Kafka looked at the world in the same way that he looked at his authoritative father and felt helpless in the face of the world. He wrote letters to this world that he could not cope with, letters that he'd never send. Max Brod did not understand

Kafka. We discussed this matter in *Axiome*, the magazine that we published during the war. Aragon, who survived the First World War, joined the Resistance during the Second World War and contributed to our magazine. That's when he told me his life story. We didn't know each other's real names, as everyone in the Resistance had an alias."

COMMISSIONER MÜLLER: "When I told Mr. Brod that he was obliged to attend the hearing, I should have been suspicious when he agreed immediately. He distracted us so that he could leave Berlin without drawing attention."

FERDY KAPLAN: "Apparently he did not want to be subjected to the prosecutor's questions and to descend into a new debate about Kafka."

COMMISSIONER MÜLLER: "I'm no longer taking into consideration the presumptions of the prosecutor. Neither the idea of a link between *Axiome* and *Stylo Noir*, nor the interference of East Germany—"

FERDY KAPLAN: "So you're thoroughly confident in your new argument."

COMMISSIONER MÜLLER: "I think that Mr. Brod did not want to be confronted with you. The dialogue that would take place between you two might have led to the disclosure of his game."

FERDY KAPLAN: "Commissioner Müller, isn't this direction of yours turning too sharply? How could such a short letter change all of your thoughts?"

COMMISSIONER MÜLLER: "Why are you surprised by this? It was you who spoke yesterday about the power of drawing long conclusions from short letters."

FERDY KAPLAN: "That's not the same thing."

COMMISSIONER MÜLLER: "If only I had changed my mind earlier, I could have stopped Mr. Brod from fleeing."

FERDY KAPLAN: "How could you have managed to change your mind? You kept focusing on the wrong spots from the very start."

COMMISSIONER MÜLLER: "Having seen a young victim on the scene and caught an assailant red-handed, I saw everything too simply and easily. Just as I ignored what you said, I also ignored some of the reports that reached us."

FERDY KAPLAN: "What reports?"

COMMISSIONER MÜLLER: "Yesterday, when I was listening to Mr. Brod's letter, I became aware of a mistake that I had made earlier. I remembered a note from the French police. They stated that it was important, but I somehow didn't find it relevant to our case."

FERDY KAPLAN: "What was it about?"

COMMISSIONER MÜLLER: "They say that letters from Tel Aviv would often be delivered to *Stylo Noir*."

FERDY KAPLAN: "From Tel Aviv?"

COMMISSIONER MÜLLER: "You're surprised, aren't you?"

FERDY KAPLAN: "I can't deny that I'm surprised."

COMMISSIONER MÜLLER: "The French police say that in those letters there were readers' comments and articles for publication."

FERDY KAPLAN: "Please, go on."

COMMISSIONER MÜLLER: "I think you and I are about to reach a point of consensus, for the first time. Before we move on, have a cigarette."

(Commissioner Müller offers Ferdy Kaplan a cigarette.)

FERDY KAPLAN: "I'm all ears."

COMMISSIONER MÜLLER: "The articles defending Kafka and criticizing Max Brod mostly came through those letters. And it was Mr. Brod himself who wrote them under a pseudonym. My logic leads me to this conclusion."

FERDY KAPLAN: "I would understand Mr. Brod suffering a crisis of conscience, but still, isn't it an extreme scenario for him to plot his own murder?"

COMMISSIONER MÜLLER: "At the time of his death Kafka was unknown, but Brod was famous. Now the situation is reversed. While everyone knows Kafka, Brod's name has been forgotten. Mr. Brod seems to have desired an honorable death to ensure that his name would shine again."

FERDY KAPLAN: "And I was the one to grant him that glory."

COMMISSIONER MÜLLER: "As I was listening to his letter in the courtroom, I remembered the note from the French police. Then I saw that it was not you but Mr. Brod himself who wrote the article in the magazine."

FERDY KAPLAN: "And at the end of his letter to the court he emphasized that he wished he had died instead of that young man."

COMMISSIONER MÜLLER: "That was his true wish, Mr. Kaplan."

FERDY KAPLAN: "Now I understand."

COMMISSIONER MÜLLER: "It also becomes clear that Mr. Brod agreed with you. He believed that he should be punished, which means he adopted your very truth."

FERDY KAPLAN: "By your argument, the opposite is in effect. It was not my truth but that of Mr. Brod, as he had spread that idea through his articles in the magazine."

COMMISSIONER MÜLLER: "Especially at the time of the surveys, readers' letters from Israel poured in. The French police initially saw that as a sign of love for Kafka being a Jewish writer and his popularity in Israel."

FERDY KAPLAN: "It may be possible. Readers from Israel showed a special interest in Kafka, and perhaps they were not very fond of Mr. Brod. Maybe the news of the survey was reported in the Israeli press and so people heard about it."

COMMISSIONER MÜLLER: "This is just an assumption, one that there is no solid basis for."

FERDY KAPLAN: "Yours is also an assumption. If Mr. Brod had been behind all this, the French police would have figured it out, wouldn't they? In the reports they shared with you, did they state Mr. Brod's direct involvement with these events?"

COMMISSIONER MÜLLER: "No, his name is not mentioned in their reports."

FERDY KAPLAN: "Here it is . . . you yourself are interpreting what they didn't say."

COMMISSIONER MÜLLER: "I understand that you find it difficult to believe. In the beginning, I too couldn't bring myself to accept the obvious facts. Now I take a totally different position."

FERDY KAPLAN: "And does the prosecutor think the same? Does he share your hypothesis?"

COMMISSIONER MÜLLER: "He hasn't heard it yet. This is something only we know, people here—you, me, and my colleagues. I have spent the whole night trying to convince them."

(Commissioner Müller looks at his fellow officers.)

FERDY KAPLAN: "It seems that your officers are finding it hard to believe you, just like me. Look at their faces."

COMMISSIONER MÜLLER: "They are tired, they need to rest. That's all."

FERDY KAPLAN: "We are all tired."

COMMISSIONER MÜLLER: "Yes, Mr. Kaplan. *(Commissioner Müller looks at his watch.)* Now go and rest for a couple of hours, then we'll come back to take you to the hearing."

FERDY KAPLAN: "I need to gather my thoughts with a clear mind, so that I'll be able to see better where you have gone wrong."

COMMISSIONER MÜLLER: "I think, today is not my day for being mistaken."

FERDY KAPLAN: "I will see you later."

COMMISSIONER MÜLLER: "Lie down and close your eyes. Even if you can't sleep, it will be good for your headache."

7 WEST BERLIN FROM THE PRISON TOWARD THE COURTHOUSE

As the city of Berlin once again bakes under the midday sun, three prison vehicles take Ferdy Kaplan to the courthouse. Due to the intense heat, everyone is either in their workplace or at home, the streets are desolate. A heavy smell of mold and damp emanates alongside the wall that splits the city.

Commissioner Müller sits next to Ferdy Kaplan in the middle vehicle of the convoy.

COMMISSIONER MÜLLER: "Did you manage to sleep?"

FERDY KAPLAN: "Only two hours? How is that possible?"

COMMISSIONER MÜLLER: "And your headache?"

FERDY KAPLAN: "It's a little less now."

COMMISSIONER MÜLLER: "Having a bit of a rest has been helpful, then."

FERDY KAPLAN: "Commissioner Müller, I see that you are slowly becoming kind toward me."

COMMISSIONER MÜLLER: "The closer one gets to the truth, the gentler one becomes. There are some secrets you haven't revealed to us, and yet we've found out what we need to know for now. Your case is unlike any other murder inquiry. Even if I know that what you did was wrong, I am still trying to understand you."

FERDY KAPLAN: "Good cop—"

COMMISSIONER MÜLLER: "No, that's not right, I am not playing the good cop, bad cop game."

FERDY KAPLAN: "Today I am believing what you say. It's all right. What about you, did you get some rest?"

COMMISSIONER MÜLLER: "You see, you are becoming kind to me too."

FERDY KAPLAN: "Day by day, I am growing in resemblance to you."

COMMISSIONER MÜLLER: "I didn't have time to rest. I was on the phone, talking with the Paris police."

FERDY KAPLAN: "Did you get anything useful from them?"

COMMISSIONER MÜLLER: "I told them that I didn't have time to wait for days on end for new reports and explained the conclusions I had arrived at. They confirmed that some of the articles for *Stylo Noir* were posted from Tel Aviv. And, during the days of the survey 'Should Max Brod pay the price?,' responses increasingly flooded in from Tel Aviv and other cities in Israel. They too think that these letters determined the outcome of the survey. Then I told them about my opinion that it was Max Brod himself who was behind all this. Even if they wouldn't be able to include this in their report yet, they said that they too share my opinion."

FERDY KAPLAN: "So they said you were right?"

COMMISSIONER MÜLLER: "Yes, they said that clearly. Mr. Kaplan, now I am hoping you too will accept that I am right."

FERDY KAPLAN: "I accept what you said."

COMMISSIONER MÜLLER: "Really?"

FERDY KAPLAN: "Yes, really."

COMMISSIONER MÜLLER: "So I have succeeded in convincing you. At last. For the first time I am one step ahead of you in this case."

FERDY KAPLAN: "We can say that, yes, you are ahead of me. But it's not your arguments that convinced me to accept your theory."

COMMISSIONER MÜLLER: "What does that mean?"

FERDY KAPLAN: "I myself found a piece of evidence that eventually convinced me."

COMMISSIONER MÜLLER: "If you didn't believe me, what changed your mind?"

FERDY KAPLAN: "No, that's not what I meant to say. I believed you, but I kept looking for a weak point in your theory, trying to find a flaw in your argument, until I myself realized something. How strange, how had I not figured it out before..."

COMMISSIONER MÜLLER: "What did you realize?"

FERDY KAPLAN: "Dante."

COMMISSIONER MÜLLER: "Dante?"

FERDY KAPLAN: "Well, it's something that I didn't pay attention to before. This morning, when I was returning to my cell after speaking with you, I walked through a dimly lit corridor, with two guards alongside me. The ceiling of the corridor was low, it felt like I was entering a tomb. The walls were filthy, the plaster was worn, and the smell of urine was everywhere. There were moans coming from behind the iron doors. As the sound of the guards' boots echoed on the concrete, I felt as if it was the sound of the demons' hooves in hell. At that moment I remembered *Inferno*, the hell in Dante's book. Mr. Brod mentioned it in his letter."

COMMISSIONER MÜLLER: "So what of it? You also mentioned Dante before. The source was the article in *Stylo Noir*, it was used there."

FERDY KAPLAN: "This morning, when you said that Mr. Brod might have been the author of that article in the magazine, my mind went blank for a while. Only later I remembered that sentence in Mr. Brod's letter."

COMMISSIONER MÜLLER: "An ordinary sentence—"

FERDY KAPLAN: "Yes, Mr. Brod said something ordinary and pronounced the name of Dante's book as *Comedy*."

COMMISSIONER MÜLLER: "I wonder what conclusion you are going to draw from this."

FERDY KAPLAN: "The name of Dante's book is *Divine Comedy*. It has been published for centuries under this title, that's how it is known."

COMMISSIONER MÜLLER: "They taught us that in high school."

FERDY KAPLAN: "They taught you wrong."

COMMISSIONER MÜLLER: "What's wrong with that?"

FERDY KAPLAN: "Dante didn't name his book *Divine Comedy*, he just called it *Comedy*. He too had a Brod figure who appeared after his death. The Italian writer Boccaccio, while giving lectures and writing papers on Dante's *Comedy*, added the word 'divine' to the title of the book. He turned *Comedy* into *Divine Comedy*."

COMMISSIONER MÜLLER: "They didn't teach us that in school."

FERDY KAPLAN: "Dante died a year after he finished *Comedy*. Boccaccio was a child at the time. He grew up, became a famous writer, and then broke the will of a dead writer by changing the name of his work."

COMMISSIONER MÜLLER: "This world of literature seems filled with strange crimes—"

FERDY KAPLAN: "Crime! You got it right, and now for the first time you begin to think like me."

COMMISSIONER MÜLLER: "By saying 'crime,' I didn't mean go and kill someone."

FERDY KAPLAN: "Boccaccio has been dead for centuries, don't worry about him."

COMMISSIONER MÜLLER: "I used to feel it was a pity I couldn't find enough time to read literature, but now I almost feel like I should be grateful that I stayed away from that world."

FERDY KAPLAN: "We should prevent the killing of the soul of a writer whose physical body isn't with us anymore, Mr. Müller. At least, bear this in mind, will you?"

COMMISSIONER MÜLLER: "If everyone does whatever they want, I don't understand, no, such a thing doesn't make sense... Imagine, a literary figure would come along and change Goethe's *Faust* one hundred years later, or two hundred years later—"

FERDY KAPLAN: "*Divine Faust!*"

COMMISSIONER MÜLLER: "I can't believe that."

FERDY KAPLAN: "It's about those Brod figures you believe in, they bring these things into being."

COMMISSIONER MÜLLER: "So do you think Mr. Brod knows what happened to Dante's book?"

FERDY KAPLAN: "Yes, he knew that Dante, like Kafka, was a victim of injustice, and in this way, he compared himself to Boccaccio. Because he felt guilty, he wrote an article in which he mentioned Dante and sent it to *Stylo Noir*. He did the same thing in the letter he sent to the court, not referring to Dante's book by its changed name, I mean he didn't use the word 'divine.' He became loyal to the author's will and called it *Comedy*. It was in this way that he showed his fidelity to the truth. I realized this when I was walking back to my cell in the dimly lit corridor, and that's when I believed that you were right."

COMMISSIONER MÜLLER: "If that's so, not even dying can save writers, anything can happen to them at any time."

FERDY KAPLAN: "Dead writers have nobody but us, the readers. Justice and mercy are in our hands, not in the courts."

COMMISSIONER MÜLLER: "You see, Mr. Brod also didn't believe in the courts. He believed in the readers, and he wanted the readers themselves to give him punishment."

FERDY KAPLAN: "Mr. Müller, do you know who I'm thinking of right now?"

COMMISSIONER MÜLLER: "Who?"

FERDY KAPLAN: "Young Ernest Fischer. I am feeling so sorry for his parents."

COMMISSIONER MÜLLER: "After the facts that you have learned now, would you still hunt down Max Brod?"

FERDY KAPLAN: "If I had the chance this time, I would go after him because of Ernest Fischer, not because of Kafka."

COMMISSIONER MÜLLER: "What happened to the tradition?"

FERDY KAPLAN: "What tradition?"

COMMISSIONER MÜLLER: "The tradition that gives a man freedom to live if the rope at the gallows has broken."

FERDY KAPLAN: "You are right, Commissioner Müller, you are quite right today. Let me ask you something. Do you think that Mr. Brod also had anything to do with the debate on Kafka, the one that appeared for the first time in *Axiome* years ago?"

COMMISSIONER MÜLLER: "He had no connection with that magazine. But he heard the debate and became aware of the survey 'Should Kafka be burned?' As he grew older, he began to question what he did, and then he remembered that debate. He took the example from there and sent that letter to *Stylo Noir*."

FERDY KAPLAN: "Is this a comment of yours? Or is that what the reports from France are saying?"

COMMISSIONER MÜLLER: "It's not in the reports, but I asked the French police about it on the phone this morning. They said that the first debate about Kafka was the idea of the people in the Resistance who published *Axiome*."

FERDY KAPLAN: "I'm glad to hear that."

COMMISSIONER MÜLLER: "You are glad to hear that? What does this matter now?"

FERDY KAPLAN: "Think of Mr. Brod, how he managed to control Kafka's fate, influenced *Stylo Noir*, and, as if that were not enough, mapped out his own death. But what you said was that there was at least one place that this man's hand couldn't reach, and so I am glad to hear that. Do you know that when Kafka was still a young man, before he published anything, Brod named Kafka among the greatest writers of the time in his article for *Die Gegenwart* magazine, published here in Berlin. Even at that early stage, he decided to etch the name of an unknown civil servant from Prague into history. Anything can be expected from a person who has such fervor."

COMMISSIONER MÜLLER: "In fact, I wouldn't have been surprised if we had even seen his fingers dabbling in *Axiome* too."

FERDY KAPLAN: "Mr. Müller, when I came out alive from the ruins during the war, I believed that anything was possible in life, and now I believe that more than ever."

COMMISSIONER MÜLLER: "I have cultivated the same belief in my profession."

FERDY KAPLAN: "I want to ask something. Do your vehicles always follow the same route? Is there no other way? If only you had gone through my neighborhood, around Steglitz or Grunewald. I wished to see those places."

COMMISSIONER MÜLLER: "What are you saying? Remember, this is a prison vehicle, not a tourist bus. Besides, you live in Steglitz, what business have you got in Grunewald?"

FERDY KAPLAN: "Both Kafka and my grandfather lived in that area."

COMMISSIONER MÜLLER: "Did Kafka live in Berlin? This is news to me. I think I should stop researching Max Brod's life and instead concentrate a little more on Kafka's life."

FERDY KAPLAN: "I found out much later on, too, that Kafka lived here. I don't know if my grandfather was actually acquainted with him, but the story he told me about Kafka, when he was seeing me off to Istanbul, was not a story that would have been known by anyone at the time."

COMMISSIONER MÜLLER: "What story is that?"

FERDY KAPLAN: "Kafka spent the final year of his life in Berlin with his lover, Dora. They lived in the Steglitz neighborhood. They were in financial difficulties and were also dealing with an awful landlord. Afterward, they moved to Grunewaldstraße."

COMMISSIONER MÜLLER: "And the story your grandfather told you..."

FERDY KAPLAN: "You're becoming more interested in stories, Mr. Müller."

COMMISSIONER MÜLLER: "How could I not, after all this."

FERDY KAPLAN: "One day, as Kafka and Dora were taking a walk in the park, they came across a little girl who was crying because she had lost her doll. Kafka tried to comfort the girl, telling her that her doll had not been lost, but that it was bored living with the same family and decided to go on a journey. 'I know this because your doll sent me a letter,' he said. The little girl looked at him in disbelief and asked him to prove it. The next day, Kafka arrived with a letter in his hand. The letters went on for three weeks, and in the final one the doll wrote that it had met a man and married him."

COMMISSIONER MÜLLER: "It seems Kafka was fond of children."

FERDY KAPLAN: "So was my grandfather. When he told me this story about Kafka, he elaborated it in his own way. In his version, Kafka came back with a doll and told the little girl that her doll had returned. By adding this ending to the story, my grandfather was trying to give me hope. But Kafka didn't try to give hope to anyone. On the contrary, he showed the suffocating side of life. I discovered the original story when I read books about Dora. It happened forty years ago, right here in this city. My grandfather was around here too, at that time."

COMMISSIONER MÜLLER: "Dora...do you think I should read up on her too?"

FERDY KAPLAN: "If you want to see someone whole-heartedly devoted to Kafka, you must know Dora. When Kafka's tuberculosis was worsening, Dora found a place for him in a sanatorium near Vienna. As he took his last breath, Dora brought him a bunch of flowers. Kafka opened his eyes, smelled the flowers...and, well..."

COMMISSIONER MÜLLER: "That's how he died?"

(The prison convoy slows down as it enters a quiet street and comes to a halt.)

FERDY KAPLAN: "Yes, that's how he died. Dora was the only person who believed that people should pay respect to Kafka himself, not to his works. For that reason, she came out against the publication of his books. She said this to Max Brod too."

COMMISSIONER MÜLLER: "Mr. Kaplan, we cannot change our route, but tomorrow I will go have a look around the places where Kafka, Dora, and your grandfather once walked, and I'll tell you what I have seen."

FERDY KAPLAN: "Thank you."

(The prison convoy remains at a standstill.)

COMMISSIONER MÜLLER: "What's up? What are we waiting for?"

(Commissioner Müller leans forward from the backseat, and sees a white minibus that is broken down and blocking the road ahead. The driver of the minibus is under the hood, busying himself with the engine. A guard from the prison van gets out and goes to give him a hand. At that moment, a few armed men jump out of the minibus's rear door. Several others pour out from a shop on the corner and join them. Some have shotguns and some have handguns. Their faces are covered by masks or scarves. They don't speak but communicate only with gestures. They apprehend the prison guard who has come to help the driver. They surround the convoy. Among them is a woman with short hair. The woman points her gun and walks confidently. She approaches the vehicle in the middle. When Commissioner Müller sees her coming, he draws his gun.)

COMMISSIONER MÜLLER: "For God's sake! What's that? Wait for my signal!"

(The two officers in the front seat also draw their guns.)

FERDY KAPLAN: "Don't try it, you have no chance."

COMMISSIONER MÜLLER: "I can see that. But I'm not going to be a sitting duck either."

FERDY KAPLAN: "Don't you see you are surrounded?"

COMMISSIONER MÜLLER: "You were expecting this, weren't you, you knew all about it."

FERDY KAPLAN: "How could I know about it? You even transferred me to a different prison. How could anyone reach out to me?"

COMMISSIONER MÜLLER: "I will find out how this happened."

FERDY KAPLAN: "I just asked you if you could change your route, only a moment ago I suggested that you go through other neighborhoods. If I had known all this, would I have said that to you?"

As he was getting used to Paris and his new life there, Ferdy's headaches began to worsen. He tried to manage with the medicines he already had, but when they became ineffective, he went to the hospital to consult Doctor Hugo. He told him that when he was a child he had been wounded in the war and had a piece of shrapnel lodged in his head. Doctor Hugo took an X-ray, examined him, and consulted with his colleagues. "You have a tumor in your brain," he said. "That is why you are having such a disturbing headache. You need to have surgery, but I have to say, it is the kind of operation that carries risks." Ferdy said that he did not want surgery and asked Doctor Hugo for a favor. "Can we please not mention a word of this to Amalya and Eliz?" Doctor Hugo agreed.

"Well, we won't tell them, but if they suspect and ask, we'll have to tell them the truth." Ferdy nodded. "You know, Doctor Hugo, Amalya told me about your family and your village. You don't seem to forget the numbers. I don't forget the numbers either. We look alike, you and me. You are following the trail of the last informant who targeted your village, you and your friends. Are you still seeking him?" Doctor Hugo said, "Yes, we are still after him. The man is moving fast, he keeps changing his location, he always manages to slip away at the last minute." Ferdy held his breath for a moment, then expressed his intention: "I would like to join your team." Doctor Hugo discouraged him. "What? In your condition? No, that is not possible." Ferdy insisted. "My health is of no importance, I want to do something with you. Actually, we both want to." Doctor Hugo was surprised. "By 'both,' do you mean you and Amalya?" he asked. "Yes," said Ferdy. Doctor Hugo approached and took Ferdy by the arm. "Let's talk about this later. Now you should go and rest."

Ferdy wandered the streets all day, alone. He hummed songs to himself. He sat on the bank of the Seine and watched the passing boats, listening to the passengers' cheerful voices. When he woke up that night, he was drenched in sweat, and he told Amalya about the dream he had been having. "It's so strange," he said. "I had a similar dream many years ago. My mother was standing in a secluded street, waiting, motionless. I was a child. I ran to her. Don't leave me alone, Mommy, I said. I was crying. My mother embraced me and told me to rest in her arms. I rested my head on her breast and that's when I woke up." Amalya put out her hand in the dark room, touching his face and kissing him gently. She wrapped her arms around his neck and said, "We shall not spend a single day away from each other, Ferdy." They slept together, they woke up together. They laughed, they wandered around. They went to the cinema, they read books.

While reading Kafka's last story, "A Hunger Artist," they decided to write letters to the dead. Writing letters to the dead was a sign of the respect they had for life. Because the Hunger Artist said "Forgive me!" before he died in Kafka's story, they wrote him a postcard with the words: "We forgive you, and you forgive us too!" They mailed the card to the publisher of the story. They wrote a card to Kafka and sent it to the address of the New Jewish Cemetery in Prague. Then it was time to write to people they knew. Ferdy wrote a card to his grandparents and sent it to the Merkezefendi Cemetery in Istanbul. He posted a card to his Berlin grandfather at Steglitz Cemetery and a card to his parents with the address of the house where they died. Amalya wrote a long letter to her father; he had been a pilot who died when she was five. She sent it to the Mediterranean Sea, where his plane had crashed in the middle of the night. The address on the envelope was simple: "The Mediterranean Sea, Middle of the Night." The rest was in the hands of the postmen.

COMMISSIONER MÜLLER: "Mr. Kaplan, I seem to have underestimated your intelligence."

FERDY KAPLAN: "I'm telling the truth. I didn't know anything about this."

COMMISSIONER MÜLLER: "No worries, now, let's get on with our work."

FERDY KAPLAN: "There is no gain for you in fighting."

COMMISSIONER MÜLLER: "Who cares about gain now?"

FERDY KAPLAN: "Please, Mr. Müller, I don't want you to be harmed."

COMMISSIONER MÜLLER: "You're thinking of me? There's no need, I'm just doing my job here."

FERDY KAPLAN: "I'm really thinking of your safety, thinking of you and your wife. Listen, an innocent student died. If you put up a fight, the same thing might happen to you. Your colleagues here will die too."

COMMISSIONER MÜLLER: "So you're not thinking of yourself then?"

FERDY KAPLAN: "I've long since stopped thinking about myself. Just take a look and see outside..."

(The commissioner wipes the sweat from his brow and looks at the two officers sitting in front of him.)

COMMISSIONER MÜLLER: "I see that we have no chance."

FERDY KAPLAN: "Don't let anyone get hurt. They've already caught one of your colleagues."

COMMISSIONER MÜLLER: "I don't want any of our men to get hurt."

FERDY KAPLAN: "If you let me go, everyone will be safe."

COMMISSIONER MÜLLER: "What about Max Brod?"

FERDY KAPLAN: "He will be safe too."

COMMISSIONER MÜLLER: "How am I supposed to believe you?"

FERDY KAPLAN: "I believe you, Mr. Müller, and I know that deep in your heart, you believe me too."

COMMISSIONER MÜLLER: "Are you talking about a police officer and a killer believing in each other?"

FERDY KAPLAN: "I'm talking about two people who understand each other and believe in each other."

COMMISSIONER MÜLLER: "Ah, how have I fallen into this situation..."

FERDY KAPLAN: "Take one step back, just once."

COMMISSIONER MÜLLER: "For you?"

FERDY KAPLAN: "No, I'll say it again, it's for your colleagues and for your wife."

COMMISSIONER MÜLLER: "Not for myself."

FERDY KAPLAN: "I know that you can sacrifice yourself, but think of the others."

COMMISSIONER MÜLLER: "I am thinking of the others."

FERDY KAPLAN: "Yes, that's the right thing. This time, if you admit that I'm right—"

COMMISSIONER MÜLLER: "I see."

FERDY KAPLAN: "Do you agree and say yes?"

COMMISSIONER MÜLLER: "Yes, Mr. Kaplan."

FERDY KAPLAN: "That's the right thing to do."

COMMISSIONER MÜLLER: "Unfortunately, it does seem to be the case."

FERDY KAPLAN: "If your men in the front would put down their guns…"

COMMISSIONER MÜLLER: "Okay, guys, put your guns down. There is no point in a fight."

FERDY KAPLAN: "I'm glad for you, really I am."

COMMISSIONER MÜLLER: "Mr. Kaplan, I feel that it's not our lives you are thinking of but the life of that woman."

(The woman with short hair comes over and holds her gun to the car window.)

FERDY KAPLAN: "Life is strange, Mr. Müller, it's really strange."

COMMISSIONER MÜLLER: "And you are a part of that strangeness, Mr. Kaplan."

FERDY KAPLAN: "We all are."

(The woman pulls the door open, sharply. "Come on, Ferdy!" she says in French. "Come on, we're going!")

COMMISSIONER MÜLLER: "Yes, she is exactly like her. If she takes her scarf off her face, it is as if Jean Seberg will appear."

FERDY KAPLAN: "This is the end of our journey, Mr. Müller."

COMMISSIONER MÜLLER: "I still don't understand, Mr. Kaplan. On the one hand, you are interested in art and literature, and on the other, in this violence."

FERDY KAPLAN: "You know, during the Nazi era people were rescued in this way from courtrooms and prisons."

COMMISSIONER MÜLLER: "The Nazis are long gone, yet you still carry on with your old habits. You don't see that the world is changing."

FERDY KAPLAN: "You say the world is changing. If only you could change with it. For instance, if only you could become a bit more like your wife, if only you could become a bit more French."

(The woman bends her head into the car. "Come on, Ferdy," she says, "we have no time.")

COMMISSIONER MÜLLER: "I see that you have already become a bit more French."

FERDY KAPLAN: "I have to go, Mr. Müller. I hope that from now on you will take care of dead writers."

COMMISSIONER MÜLLER: "Only people like you can take care of those writers, Mr. Kaplan. My wife is a good reader, she can take care of them. There is no need for guns."

(The woman leans into the car curiously. She looks Commissioner Müller in the eye. Then she touches

Ferdy Kaplan on his right temple and asks, "Are you all right?" And without waiting for an answer, she grabs Ferdy's handcuffed hands and pulls him out of the car.)

FERDY KAPLAN: "Farewell, Mr. Müller."

COMMISSIONER MÜLLER: "Perhaps we will meet again, Mr. Kaplan."

FERDY KAPLAN: "Who knows…"

8 TOWARD THE END

*

With Ferdy Kaplan on board, the white minibus dives into the streets and disappears from sight into this city of long, silent walls.

*

Two months later, a postcard with Ernest Fischer's name on it arrives at the cemetery where he was laid to rest. On the front of the card is a hand-drawn sketch of a fishing boat, a flock of seagulls, and a cracked sun. On the back are some lines of the poet Aragon, descending like the rungs of a ladder:

I am going to tell you a great secret
Time is you
…

Time
like an endless mane of hair
Combed
A mirror that breath mists and demists
Time is you
who sleeps at dawn while I awaken
It is you like a knife across my throat
…

I am going to tell you a great secret
Shut the doors
It is easier to die than to love
That's why I give myself to the misery of living
My love

*

The same day, an envelope addressed to Commissioner Müller arrives at the police station on Friesenstraße, with a book inside: *Divine Comedy*. The word "Divine" is crossed out with red pen. An inscription is written with the same pen on the first page:

"To Mrs. Müller and Mr. Müller, for the beauty of art and kindness of people…"

*

A few months later, on December 20, Max Brod closes his eyes for the final time and passes away in Tel Aviv. In his will, he leaves his entire archive, including Kafka's works, to his secretary, asking her to donate them to a public institution. His secretary disobeys his will and transfers all the works to her private ownership, and when she dies, she bequeaths them to her daughters. For the next fifty years, there will be disputes and legal cases over Mr. Brod's will.

Shortly after his passing, a postcard arrives at Max Brod's grave in Trumpeldor Cemetery. On the front of the card is a hand-drawn portrait of Kafka and on the back, just four words:

"I love you, Max."

ABOUT THE AUTHOR

BURHAN SÖNMEZ is the author of six novels, which have been translated into forty-eight languages and received international prizes including the EBRD Literature Prize and Vaclav Havel Library Award. Sönmez was born in Turkey and grew up speaking Kurdish and Turkish. He worked as a lawyer in Istanbul before going into political exile in Britain. His writing has appeared in such publications as *The Guardian*, *La Repubblica*, and *Der Spiegel*. *Lovers of Franz K.* is the first novel he was written in his mother tongue, Kurdish. His previous novels include *Labyrinth* (Other Press, 2019) and *Stone and Shadow* (Other Press, 2023). He is president of PEN International and a Senior Member of Hughes Hall College and Trinity College, University of Cambridge. He lives in Cambridge and Istanbul.

ABOUT THE TRANSLATOR

SAMÎ HÊZIL is a writer and translator from northern Kurdistan. He holds a bachelor's degree in English language and literature, and has been translating literary and scientific works from English into Kurdish since 2000. His short stories and scholarly articles in Kurdish have been published by a variety of literary publications. He teaches Kurdish literature at Kurdî-Der (The Kurdish Language Association) in Van, Turkey.